THE RETURN OF THE AMAZING BULK

A NOVEL BY
ATOM MUDMAN BEZECNY

BASED ON THE FILM CREATED BY
LEWIS SCHOENBRUN, KEITH SCHAFFNER, AND JEREMIAH CAMPBELL

Encyclopocalypse Publications
www.encyclopocalypse.com

THE RETURN OF THE AMAZING BULK

Second Edition, 2025
ISBN: 978-1-966037-38-5
Cover Art Copyright © 2021 James Bezecny

Layout and design by Sean Duregger
Interior formatting by Sean Duregger
Edited by Katherine Avalon, Michael Kobold, and Mike Watt

ACKNOWLEDGMENTS

It is often said that no book is produced in a vacuum, and this is 100% true. Books can only emerge from living, breathing environments, and no author is completely responsible for the creation of their work.

I would like to thank Lewis Schoenbrun, Keith Schaffner, and Jeremiah Campbell for giving me the great opportunity to write and publish this story.

Many thanks, as ever, to my brother James, as without his tremendous artistic talent the cover of this book would not exist.

Thank you to Katherine Avalon and Michael Kobold, for assisting me in the editing of this book and for helping to make Odd Tales Productions into a stellar publishing house.

And more thanks than I can count to my astounding partner, the love of my life, the light of my soul, Julian—this book is dedicated to him, that amazing man who will always be my personal superhero.

-Atom Mudman Bezecny

There can be no great superman.

> — DR. FRANCIS ARDAN IV, IN AN ADDRESS TO
> THE UNITED NATIONS, 1997

god, it's good that life's an effervescent toy
for all work and no play make Jack a dull boy

> — SELECTION FROM "JACK" BY J. TORRANCE
> (TYPEWRITER LEAVES, PENGUIN BOOKS,
> POSTHUMOUS PUBLICATION)

THE RETURN OF
THE AMAZING
BULK

CHAPTER 1

Hannah Darwin sat in her large mansion staring out the front window at the exquisite fountain her father, the recently deceased General Darwin, had bought for their family long ago. It was probably a gift for her late mother, she considered, almost absent-mindedly. She wasn't *really* looking at the fountain—she wasn't really looking at anything. Her mind felt numb, as she mourned a death beside her father's. It had all happened on that awful night, just three nights prior. Another man had met his death besides the General: the man who was the love of her life. His name was—

"Hank!" Hannah exclaimed. She felt the touch of a hand on her shoulder and with a short gasp, her head snapped around. She spat the name out reflexively upon seeing the face of the young man who stared at her through the darkness of her living room.

Even though his name escaped her lips, it took her a moment to realize it was really him. His dark eyes stared at her from between his long tresses of dark hair. His face wore the pained scowl she had last seen him carry. She embraced him immediately.

"How—how did—?" This was the second time now that her

fiancé had escaped death. First she thought he had died in the line of duty, caught in a bomb-blast stopping some mad scientist named Kantlove. That was what her father had told her, but she knew now she shouldn't have trusted the General.

"It was that blasted serum," Hank Howard growled. "The chemicals that turned me into that—that thing. That *Bulk*."

"Hank, what are you talking about?" Hannah asked. "Your father wanted me to create a serum to turn people into super-soldiers," he said. "I succeeded—but in doing so I used the serum on myself. I became a colossal purple beast, unable to control the boiling wrath within me."

"And it brought you back to life?!" she gasped.

"Yes. I rose from my grave to find myself with a faceful of urine," Hank said bitterly. "It was a dumb detective who'd been hounding me, some loser named Garton."

"I heard about him on the news," Hannah said. "I heard that you—that the Bulk—squashed his partner."

"In retrospect I can understand his anger," admitted Hank. "But the point is, waking up to a yellow shower pissed me off. I lost control, and became the Bulk. I gave him a conk on the head, and he lapsed into a coma. I guess when he woke up, he had amnesia. Couldn't remember anything at all."

"So your secret is safe," Hannah mused.

"Listen—Hannah—I realize now that we can never be together. I just wanted to say goodbye, before I disappear forever. I have a monster inside me, and I killed your father! You could never forgive me."

She shrugged. "Let's face it, my dad was a major jerk. Well, technically, a General jerk. I cried for maybe a couple hours, smoked a joint, and then I whipped out a calculator and added up all my inheritance. If you wanted to stay here, Hank, we wouldn't have to worry about anything for—I think at least 42 years. And that's even if we live it up a little bit."

"Hannah—you're serious?" asked Hank.

"My feelings for you haven't changed. And they never will,

darling." And she kissed him firmly on the lips—a tingle rose through his whole body.

"I love you, Hannah."

"And I love you, Hank."

They grinned widely at each other.

"I do need a place to hide," Hank confessed. "I need to find a way to control the Bulk. And for that I'll need scientific equipment..."

"Why don't we go talk to your friend Sam?"

"Y-yeah, he could help..." Hank said. "I lost track of Sam after all of this. I don't think he knows what happened to me."

"You guys were getting funding from the government—there's no way he got away scot-free!" realized Hannah. "Oh, Hank, we need to go to the lab. Sam could be in danger!"

"You're right," Hank nodded sullenly. "Let's go right away!"

"Wait, Hank—you can't go out in public. You're supposed to be dead!" Hannah was lost in thought for some time. Then, a grin broke out across her face. "I have an idea. Follow me."

She took Hank by the arm and led him down into her family's wine cellar. Before the large casks of wine was a shelf of bottling supplies; she perused it until she found a small jar, labeled, "GENERAL DARWIN'S SPARE MUSTACHES—AUTHORIZED PERSONNEL ONLY!"

She carefully extracted one of the mustaches and attached it to Hank's upper lip. "There— perfect," she said.

"We can't waste any time!" Hank cried.

"You're right. I'll drive. Porsche, or Lamborghini?" Hank didn't answer. She chose the Bugatti.

It wasn't a long drive to the lab—maybe fifteen minutes or so. As they traveled, Hank said, "Hannah, there's still so much I have to say to you."

"I have a lot to say to you—and a lot to do, as well."

He smiled thinly. "Yes. Well. It's just—I want to know if you still want to marry me."

"Hank—I need some time to think. I've never been engaged to a dead man before."

"I mean, I'm not *actually* dead—"

"I know," she said, "but there's paperwork and stuff to figure out. I know you went through Hell, darling, and back again, but I—"

"Do you still love me?"

"Of course I still love you. I'm just a little mixed up right now."

"It's okay," he said, "I know the feeling."

Soon they were outside the laboratory. To Hank's surprise it actually looked worse than it had the last time he saw it—the lab had never exactly been a pretty sight. For one, the city had pretty much let this neighborhood go to waste. The ugly yellowish structure had needed a new coat of paint sometime back when kids played with lawn darts. The ground floor windows had bars over them. The one ordinary door was electronically bolted, linked to a battered and imposingly large keypad. There were actually more facilities connected to this sore thumb of a building, consisting of shorter bunkers stretching out into the heart of the block. These were hidden behind thick concrete containment walls.

Hank and Hannah could see at once that getting in was easier said than done. There was police tape everywhere, and large men in suits and sunglasses guarded all the entrances. Hank and Hannah exchanged a look.

"You stay here," Hank urged.

"Nothing doing. If you want us to get married, I suggest you get used to the idea of me as an action girl."

He could only nod at that. They exited the car, and approached the colossal guards.

"Hello," Hank said awkwardly, through gritted teeth, "My name is...Homer. I am an employee at this lab..."

"Sir, I'm afraid this lab is under lockdown right now," the man in black said. "Who is this woman?"

"I'm, uh—I'm his wife, Marge," Hannah said.

"I see. Well, unfortunately, you two, all access to this building has been suspended for the time being."

Hank sensed that Sam was in danger. He had studied the parking lot as they pulled in, and one uncomfortable fact stood out to him: his coworkers' cars were still here. Including Sam's.

"Listen, I'm going in whether you want me to or not," said Hank. And he tried to force his way past the two men. They squeezed in tight and tried to shove him back, but he dug his heels in. They were forced to push him off his feet, and slammed back hard on the pavement. Hannah couldn't stop herself.

"Hank! Er—I mean—Homer!"

"Hank?" one of the agents said. "As in Hank Howard—? Hey, Bob, we can't let this one escape!"

"Steve, that can't be Hank Howard. This man has a mustache!" the second agent exclaimed. "Maybe we *should* let him in..."

"You should," Hank said, "for your own safety."

"That's a threat!" cried the first agent. "Club him! We're taking him to a detention center!"

"I wouldn't...recommend that," Hank said. He turned to look at Hannah. "Get back, darling. Get far back."

He grunted, and suddenly a spark of lightning flashed through his eyes. Purple lightning.

"What are you gonna do, Howard?" said one of the agents. Fear broke into his voice.

"*I* don't have any say in the matter. *He* just comes out when he smells rage." Hank stepped away from them, and at once, a tornado seemed to swoop around his body. Trash and dust swirled around in the rush of wind, and purple lightning bolts crackled within the storm's viciousness. Hannah and the two agents shielded their eyes against this sudden tempest, their hair billowing wildly in the wind.

When the tornado cleared, Hank was gone. In his place was a colossus of churning purple flesh. The naked behemoth stood over 14 feet tall—its corpulent body swayed unsteadily as if rocking in the breeze. With tiny eyes, the Bulk stared at the two guards, who trembled before him. He swung his hand back, and with a single swipe he brushed the two guards aside. He was too small for the front door, but he'd soon remedy that. He pulled his fist back again, and with one titanic punch he smashed the front of the building in, with a roar of shattered concrete.

"Hank! Hank, no!" Hannah shouted. The Bulk paid her no mind. She mused aloud, "It's no use, he's not Hank anymore."

But as she said this, the Bulk turned to look at her. Fear flooded her heart. She was certain the creature was going to attack her. He couldn't, could he? Some part of Hank deep inside him would hold him back...

He made no move against her. Instead, he seemed to be waiting anxiously for her to speak again.

"Remember what we're here to do, Hank!" she called. "Sam! We're here for Sam, remember?"

The Bulk shook his head, but not in refusal. He was trying to make sense of her words. Eventually, however, he turned back towards the laboratory, whose front wall was decimated. More guards were on their way over, at top speed.

The Bulk released a loud, bestial roar, and charged into the lab. Not wanting to be arrested, Hannah followed him in, watching him smash his way through his former place of employment. It wasn't long before it became a disaster. Electrical equipment and chemicals spilled all over the ground, and before they knew it, this tenuous mixture lit up in a series of explosions. The building was coming down around their ears.

The government agents—if that's what they were—paid no attention to her. They sprinted into the ruins, opening fire on the Bulk with all different types of guns. But the bullets bounced off, even the heaviest types—the Bulk barely noticed them as he tore apart brick and mortar in his hunt for his friend. Hannah managed to stay off to the side, keeping herself hidden.

She knew Hank had made a lot of memories in this laboratory. She wondered if he would regret tearing it down like this.

But he calmed down once he punched open a hole into one of the rooms. He growled, and wavered before the opening. Hannah wasn't far behind him, and she peered inside to see what he was looking at. Immediately, she saw a group of about twenty people bound and gagged, roped to chairs. She didn't recognize any of them except for Sam, who stared in horror at the colossus standing before him. After a moment the Bulk reached inside to grab Sam, who would have screamed if there wasn't a gag in his mouth. He flailed wildly as the purple beast delicately removed him from the chair, and hauled him over his shoulder. Then the giant creature turned to look at Hannah. He grabbed her as well, though she was a bit more prepared for this than Sam. He rushed away from the other hostages, back into the banks of men who swarmed through the hallways.

When it's time to carry me over the threshold, I hope he takes a different approach! Hannah thought to herself.

She and Sam watched helplessly as the Bulk plowed over the crowds of armed men, who were helpless against him. He ran out of the ruins of the laboratory into the streets, heedless of the vehicles that stood in his way—a single touch from his foot and the cars hurled away from them, slamming mightily into the walls of nearby buildings.

"Hannah?!" exclaimed Sam then. He'd gotten his gag loose. "What's going on? I haven't seen you since Hank died—"

"It's a long story," she shouted back at him.

"I hope this big guy knows this is coming out of our taxes!" Hannah wondered how Sam could joke at a time like this.

But then she looked ahead, and her heart sank. History was about to repeat itself, with horrifying familiarity. She had seen the stories that a chopper for a local news station was destroyed by the Bulk's previous rampage. Now a small *fleet* of news copters from the city's McGee Media Company hovered before them. The

Bulk's rage was beyond control, and as his temper grew, so did his size. To Hannah's amazement, he reared up to the height of a small building. A pitiless roar echoed out, shaking the air around the helicopters.

He was going to destroy them.

"Hank!" she cried, knowing her words would be futile. "Hank, you can't do this! Stop!"

But these pilots had more sense than the ones who had gone down before. They pulled their copters back from the rushing creature, save for one bulky craft which didn't jerk away in time. The Bulk, now a 30-foot tall titan, embraced the craft and squeezed it tight in his grip. Hannah and Sam screamed as they heard the sound of warping metal.

The machine's motor began to sputter and die, and the Bulk held it tight until all sound ceased. Then he tossed the smashed vehicle far away—it exploded with a deafening burst, and from above, a cry broke out among the reporters: "The cargo robot is down! Repeat, he blew up the cargo robot!"

This was apparently their cue to retreat. They flew off towards the horizon, vanishing from Hannah and Sam's view. The Bulk wasn't done yet, though. His enormous ears heard the sound of incoming planes.

Straight ahead was a giant skyscraper, the tallest in the city. At once the Bulk charged towards its base, and with a swift gesture, moved his two captives into one hand. The two were awkwardly squished together.

"Ohh, boy, this is too close for comfort," Sam said. "Yeah, I like my personal space," Hannah grunted.

Then, the Bulk began to climb. Sam, forever the acrophobe, began to scream shrilly. Hannah tried to cover her ears but her arms were pinned.

"The big guy's not really going to do this...?" she asked herself. "This city's going to get a flashback to the '30s...or was it the '70s?"

Once he was up at the top, the Bulk, with Hannah and Sam still in hand, began to beat his chest vigorously. A deep, guttural roar erupted from his throat. The planes were closing in. The scene was set.

The planes opened fire on the Bulk, but their accuracy was woefully poor. Snarling like a wild beast, the Bulk swatted at the planes as they closed in on him. Hannah and Sam pinched their eyes shut as they waved through the air, still pinned inside the purple giant's hand. The planes swooped around and tried another barrage of bullets, but they entirely missed the building, whose width was comparable to the broad side of a barn. To their credit, the Bulk's accuracy wasn't much better—he didn't hit a single plane.

The fight ended not with a gory victory over the Bulk or the destruction of the planes—it was just that the fighters' guns ran out of bullets. They darted off and left the city, and if planes had tails and legs, their former would be tucked between the latter.

This provoked another triumphant roar from the Bulk. Sam was still cowering from the extreme height, and once bullets came into the picture he'd gotten green around the gills. Hannah felt pity for him. She shouted, "Take us down from here, Mr. Eighth Wonder of the World!"

The Bulk complied, but probably out of his own choice than Hannah's suggestion. He jumped back to the street and, to the surprise of all, they all lived. He didn't even squash anyone on the way down, though the pavement had definitely seen better days (it wasn't always crater-shaped).

The Bulk continued his rampage, but it was clear now that escape was his goal. He sprinted from block to block, and didn't stop until he left the city—all in his path was trampled to rubble. Wreckage dotted the streets, and smoke filled the air from scattered fires.

There was a forest ahead, and the Bulk sped for it. He was losing size with every step, and eventually he had to drop his two passengers. He halted in his tracks. He was now only seven feet tall. He panted raggedly, like a large dog. Eventually, he was forced to let Sam and Hannah go. Then, at once, a tornado began to billow around him. The winds swept into close and swallowed him up, as both observers shielded their eyes. Before long this storm cleared, and standing before them was Hank Howard. To Sam's shock, he was alive; to both his and Hannah's shock, he was wearing his birthday suit.

"Oh God, I forgot this part," Hank said, shielding himself appropriately.

Hannah's eyes were wide. Hank being nude was something of a rare occurrence. She focused especially on the striped tattoo that adorned his left arm. She'd always been fond of that.

"Hank!" Sam shouted. "You're—"

"Yes, I'm naked," Hank said.

Sam said, "No, I mean you're alive!"

"Of course I'm alive. What did they tell you about me?"

"A lot of lies," said Sam with a sneer. "That you stole our formula. That you betrayed our country, and died in the effort."

"Well, I'm not dead. Doesn't make the other two accusations seem valid."

"I never believed them, Hank. Well—I believed that you were dead. I didn't want to believe that, but I did. But as far as the other stuff...I knew you wouldn't steal that formula. You needed to present it to General Darwin."

"I mean, I suppose in retrospect, I did steal the formula. I injected it into myself."

"I can see that," Sam said. "You stupid jerk! You could've gotten yourself killed."

"But I didn't."

"No." Sam shook his head, and then mellowed. "I'm glad you're alive."

"Hey, me too."

And they shook hands. Though Sam shot an awkward glance at Hank's nudity.

"You know, I'd love to talk more about everything that's happened, but, uh…" Hank looked down. "It's kind of a chilly this time of year, isn't it?"

Hannah nodded. "Sam, let's see if we can find some leaves big enough to cover up our little Tarzan here."

CHAPTER 2

A tall woman surveyed the bombed-out ruins of Castle Kantlove. The once-proud spires, which had served the Kantlove family for countless generations, were now simple mounds of stone. The bricks of this palace of a now-dead bloodline had contained a maze of hidden artwork encoded with cryptographic meaning— and now, all of that hard work had been lost. This castle was one of a kind, and it was gone forever, smashed to pieces in a rain of Air Force missiles.

As the woman made her way down into the valley where the ruins slept, she reviewed what she knew about the deceased owner of this fallen fortress. Dr. Kantlove, born Werner Ludwig Merkwürdigliebe von Kantlove in 1964, was a ruthless German mad scientist obsessed with destroying national monuments. He had a marked obsession with the phallic efficiency of cruise missiles, which almost certainly had nothing to with the origins of his family's name, and the curse which inevitably afflicted the males of his bloodline. The woman had known Kantlove through his wife Lolita Schiller, her childhood friend. She had heard much of Kantlove's boundlessly tedious attempts to win Lolita's favor— the woman smiled fondly upon thinking of her dead friend, who took pleasure in being a hard woman to please. The doctor's wealth and taste for destruction only barely sated the ravenous Lolita. The woman remembered that occasionally her bond with Lolita had exceeded friendship, and she herself had known some of the young woman's physical passion.

But now both Lolita and Kantlove were dead—these ruins a testament to their failure. The woman hadn't come to pay her respects. She hoped that the underground sections of this castle still contained some of Kantlove's weapons. The mad doctor had had his chance, and now it was *her* turn to take over the world. She'd spread her influence over the world like her name implied.

She called herself Pam Demic. She caught the eye for a multitude of reasons. Her height and defined muscles made her physical presence uncanny, while her soft bronze hair, beguiling eyes, gentle lips, and general physique rendered her a natural weapon against those attracted to women. She was dressed professionally, but her pale clothes were suited for adventure and so they clung close to her body. That body radiated strength—it was a wonder that the ground didn't crack under her feet. And yet she walked like a shadow, a thing of myth.

Scattered around these ruins were skeletons clad in Roman-style armor. Pam allowed herself a slight smile, as she savored Kantlove's hypocrisy. He had sought to unmake the ancient world by smashing its remnant wonders, and yet he was fond of the castles of Old Europe and the brutal efficiency of the Imperial Roman legions. She thought of her own Romans, her loyal servants Gaetano and Massillo. Together with her Greek henchman Petrakis, they were monitoring her life-signs from afar, making sure that nothing went wrong. Though she had warned them that this was likely going to be a boring watch. Just a lot of rubble and dead guys.

The interesting stuff, if there was any, was going to be down below. She just needed to find some sort of ingress into the catacombs.

At the center of the castle, below a layer of wreckage, Pam spotted a black shape. Her arms worked furiously to lift the broken cobbles off of this structure, her hopes growing with each stone she removed. Just what she needed: a hatch. It was locked, but she made short work of the seal with the tools she kept in her pocket. Hauling it upward, she saw only ceaseless blackness below. The electrical lights which had sustained this place were all wrecked when the missiles came down.

Still, Pam had better tools than just lock picks. She put in her dark-proof contacts and at once the tunnel below lit up. She cracked her knuckles and descended.

The air was stale, but she'd rather expected that—strange chemical smells wafted through the air, implying hidden leakages. More armor-clad skeletons dotted these tunnels, many of them clearly having died while trying to flee the complex. It was like a cemetery, and that made Pam feel right at home.

She stood in a long corridor, which was lined with the doors too many laboratories. Slowly and methodically she worked her way through the labs one by one, finding most of them stripped clean or bombed out. It didn't take long for her to realize there were footprints in the ashes—recent ones. She wasn't alone down here.

She wondered if perhaps other super villains, ex-comrades of Kantlove, had come down here to plunder their late compatriot's stores. She looked for clues of who could have done it, but nothing caught her eye.

This was getting tedious. She considered the possibility that Kantlove had over exaggerated the scope of his experiments. That made sense, given his compensatory nature. But that there was nothing here at all was undeniably disappointing.

There was only one last lab to open up: Lab O. Pam frowned. "Lab O"? But all these other labs were numbered. It wasn't Lab 0. That was when she saw that soot covered most of the door. She brushed it aside, and looked at the exposed text:

LAB OMEGA Ω

"Now we're getting somewhere," she murmured.

Stepping through the door, she saw an immediate shift in her surroundings. While the rest of the base was dead and ruined, this room was lit with an unusual green light. Pam temporarily removed her special contacts and inspected the room carefully. The green lights were coming from the humming bases of a series of glass tubes that flanked the walls. Inside these tubes was a bubbling, semi-clear liquid. Most of them seemed empty—others had lost their lights, and the faint hum that surrounded the other tubes was absent. Disappointment once more flooded Pam's heart —but then, at the far end of the room, she discovered that one of the tubes was broken. She squatted down to inspect the broken capsule and observed that its broken glass extended *outside* of the tube. To her trained eye that indicated that whatever was stored in this container had broken *out*, rather than breaking *in*.

As soon as this thought passed Pam's mind, she felt a strong arm loop around her throat from behind.

A British accent spoke in her ear. "Well, well, well—let's viddy what the koshka's dragged in, shall we?"

"Who are you?" Pam asked. Her voice was level and calm; this was far from the first chokehold someone had got on her.

"Aww, she wants to know our eemyas, darling—and she hasn't even seen you yet."

"Who are you talking—" Pam cut herself off. There was a figure emerging from the darkness, one who had managed to elude even Pam's keen eyesight. Despite her years of rigorous training, Pam Demic's eyes widened upon seeing her mysterious host.

The figure seemed at first to be an ordinary woman. Pam assumed the greenish tinge of her skin was an effect of the lighting, but as she neared her she saw that in truth her skin itself was green, a pale sea-green. Her long dark hair swept down over one shoulder—and that hair, upon closer inspection, looked more like the mycelial strands of fungi than what commonly crowned the human head. Her eyes were diamond shaped, and lacked both pupils and irises, instead being only seas of murky yellow. When she grinned, Pam saw a coral reef of fangs, which parted briefly to reveal a snaking, garishly-long tongue.

Before Pam could speak again, this creature waved her hand as if to dismiss her attacker. The strong arm parted from her throat. Pam spun around and found herself looking at a young woman clad in white, with a black bowler hat. She wore a grin as sinister as the creature's.

Pam's strong hands snapped out to grab her throat. Her eyes widened, and she jerked her closer, knocking her hat off in the process. She lifted her four inches off the ground with just one hand. As she struggled in her grip, she murmured, "I guess the tables have turned, haven't they?"

"Wait. Release her. She is useful to me," said the mysterious creature.

"Why should I care?"

"Because we could be allies. You don't know what I could do for you. I can destroy your enemies—give them a lingering death. I am Dr. Kantlove's greatest bioweapon."

Pam lifted the white-clad woman a little higher before throwing her down. She turned, and glared angrily at the creature.

"Who are you?"

"My name is Vyrass," she said. "Emphasis on the latter syllable." She turned around, revealing what was indeed a generous posterior. She waggled this back and forth, seemingly to entice her guest.

Pam was not lacking in Sapphic tendencies, but she couldn't help but raise a skeptical eyebrow, questioning once again the preferences of the late Werner von Kantlove.

"What is it you do? I mean, besides...that?"

"I told you," the entity said, "I am a bioweapon."

"But what do you *do*?"

Vyrass turned around, her grin still present. "I told you, my name is *Vyrass*. That sort of implies I have something to do with *disease*, doesn't it?"

Pam's curiosity was piqued, and that was a dangerous thing indeed. Vyrass kept talking. "My comrade is the last surviving member of the Kantlove gang. Her name is Alexis Legrande, and she, as I said, is very useful to me—"

"I have come here for a simple purpose, simpleton," Pam barked. The smaller woman seemed to flinch away from her. "I came here to claim what remained of Dr. Kantlove's arsenal, and that means you're coming with me. Bring your white-suited servant if you wish. But we have plans to make."

Instead of sinking into fear, Vyrass steadied herself and broadened her grin. "I've been waiting a long time to hear those words. I was made to fulfill evil desires. What sort of plans are you talking about?"

Pam smiled, but only for a moment. She beckoned her two newfound minions to move closer.

CHAPTER 3

In the park outside the city, Hannah and Sam managed to get Hank some leaves to cover himself. Just moments after restoring his decency, however, they heard the sounds of rustling in the bushes. Hannah raised a hand.

"We're being watched," she whispered. She carried a trace of her father's military instinct. Hank agreed with her, and they looked around for whoever was spying on them.

It didn't take long for the unseen visitor to reveal themselves. They strode out of the bushes and at once took all their breath away. She was a tall woman, and strong—her muscles were pronounced even through her soft skin. Her hair was a short mohawk dyed a radiant blue. She wore black athletic gear, which had granted her some degree of camouflage in the forest shadows. Her face was pretty but hardened—she was a little older than the three of them.

"Sorry to scare you guys," she said. "But I wanted to find somebody. I think that giant purple guy, the Bulk, is around here somewhere." She frowned. "Why are you almost naked?" she asked Hank.

"I-I..." Hank couldn't come up with an excuse.

"Doesn't matter," the woman said. "I'm ex-Drill Sergeant Blue. Retired from the U.S. Marine Corps. Nice to meet you all."

"I'm Hannah—" Hannah began, but she was interrupted by Sam, who murmured his name enthusiastically at the newcomer.

"'M Sam..." he said.

Hannah saw a strange look in Sam's eyes—he was gazing at Blue's muscles, instantly smitten.

Hank said nothing. Blue stared at him and smiled, tilting her head curiously.

"Have you seen the Bulk?" she asked him. "I want to be sure I can believe my eyes. You know I *swear* I saw him."

"We—we haven't seen it," said Hannah. "Promise we haven't." She bit her tongue then. There was no way this lady wouldn't see right through her.

"That's really interesting, y'know? Like there's a set of footprints back at the park edge leading right to where you're sitting," Blue said.

Hank still couldn't speak, so Hannah looked to Sam—but he was similarly mute. A mist had settled over his eyes and he was grinning faintly, his mind lost in fantasies of being carried off by rugged valkyries. Hannah rolled her eyes.

"Listen, do they teach you to ask all these questions as a...as a drill instructor?" Hannah asked.

"Part of being an instructor is learning the individual strengths and weaknesses of recruits," Blue said. "I guess I haven't exactly let go of doing that."

"Well, what do you want?"

"I told you. I want to know if the Bulk came through here." Her eyes hadn't shifted from staring at Hank. "Ever since I learned the Bulk existed, I've had need of him."

"Who could *use* a monster like that?" Hank asked at once. His words came out in a flash of spittle. Now Blue raised a dyed eyebrow.

"You guys are acting *really* weird. Are you on drugs or something?"

"You just caught us at a bad time," Hannah insisted.

"I think you came across us at just the right time," Sam said then, suddenly snapping back to normal form. "We could use a strong woman like you, to help keep us safe."

"Safe?" Blue asked. "Safe from what?"

"Sam, you need to relax," Hannah urged. "Listen, Ms. Blue, we're fine. We're just a little on edge right now with some personal business."

"The personal business of how this guy in the leaves is the Bulk?" The tall woman laughed. "Come on, there's literally no other reason for you to be naked. Not as long as the other two have their clothes on."

Hank frowned. "I'm not the Bulk."

"Come on, you are." Blue's grin widened, but wavered. She was holding something back. "You can tell me! I won't tell a soul, not even the military. I left that behind because I don't agree with them anymore. The Marines aren't what they used to be—they've grown harder, darker. As if they ever had that much light and love to them. As if they haven't almost always been put to horrific use."

Hank stared. "What if I was this...creature? What does that matter to you?"

"Like I said, I would have a *job* for you," Blue replied. "Darn it, can't you see I don't want this? I'm trying to separate this thing from me!"

Hank realized too late what he'd said, but he didn't care. His cover was blown from the moment she walked up to them, and it was time to face the consequences.

Blue looked down with disappointment on her face. "That's too bad. I was hoping..."

"Hoping what?" Hank cried. "The last time people had 'a job' for me, they sent me off to fight for your stupid military! I nearly died...in fact, I did die, for a little bit."

"It's *family* business," Blue said then. "I want to ask the Bulk's help to protect my grandfather."

Hannah looked at Hank then, her face full of concern.

Sam's enthusiasm only grew.

"You gotta help this lady, Hank!" he exclaimed. "We can't ignore the request of a woman in need."

"Your friend is a knight gallant, Bulk," said Blue teasingly.

But her humor faded at once. "My grandfather used to be a big man in the Mafia. I know that's not the best point for me to start with, but he's moved past his old life. He's trying to make amends now. The only issue is that some of his old comrades feel they have some unfinished business."

"How do I know that your grandpa's reformed?" Hank asked.

At once Blue's face became desperate. "I can give you nothing but my plea. I-I've been to the police, but they've been useless, as always...and none of my Marine buddies want to get involved because of what it'll mean for their careers."

Hank sighed.

"I mean, if things go downhill, the purple guy won't like it. And he's not someone you want to annoy."

"I won't let things go downhill," Blue said. "I just want to keep my grandpa safe." She sniffed. "I don't even know why I'm asking. It was just a fantasy I had, when I saw you on the news. I-I never thought I'd ever have a chance to talk to you."

Sam looked hard at Hank. "You *have* to help her," he implored. "Have a heart, man!"

"I'm starting to think the same thing, Hank," Hannah added.

"Sam, can I have a word?" Hank asked. "Excuse us, ladies." He took Sam a short distance into the woods.

"I know you have a thing for this woman...despite having just met her," Hank said. "But I'm not gonna let you and Hannah talk me into becoming that...that *monster* again. What if I kill you this time?"

"You didn't kill us last time! And trust me, you had plenty of opportunity!" Sam exclaimed. "Listen, yeah, it's true, I fall in love at first sight real easy. But I think that maybe helping an old man is what you need. Surely you can see that this power can be used for good?"

Hank looked away. "I don't believe that. And I know that because—because Hannah's feelings for me are changing. She's scared of the Bulk. I can sense it."

"Maybe helping this woman's grandpa will help her feel more comfortable with him. Who says you can't just help Blue's grandpa and *then* give up the Bulk?" Sam said. "I promise, buddy, we'll fix you up. I don't want you to worry. But I do think you should help this girl. And *not* just because she's exactly my type."

Hank didn't like it, but he was convinced. This woman was a stranger, but he was just as willing to aid a stranger as a friend.

"Fine," he said. "Let's go back and I'll tell her I'll do it."

"Aw, yes! Then we get to hang out," Sam said. "Just the four of us."

When they reentered, Blue was tapping her foot.

"So are you guys gonna help me? I was just telling your girl friend, I've got my dad's skill with a sax, I can play you some rousing tunes in battle..."

"You don't need to convince me any further, Blue," Hank said. "We'll help you."

"Thank you!" Blue exclaimed, surprised. "I'm indebted to you. If—if you have time, we can plan..."

"Yeah, yeah..." Hank said, "let's get on with it." And he looked firmly at Hannah. "Then, we're gonna work on getting this purple palooka out of me."

* * *

Meanwhile, back in the city, a man woke up in his hospital bed. Detective Ray Garton had been sleeping longer at night since his accident, which worried his physician, Dr. Will Hartford. But because Garton was unable to return to work at the police department, it could have been that this extra sleep was simply a product of his long need for a rest. Just in case,

Dr. Hartford was keeping an eye on him 24/7, sleeping or awake. Now, Hartford stood over his patient, as he did every time he awoke.

"How do you feel, Ray?" he asked.

"Hey, doc, it's not that I'm ungrateful," Garton groaned, "but you're sounding like a broken record."

He massaged his neck, and the handsome doctor watched with concern. "Does that hurt, Ray?"

"A little, but not too bad. I've got other things on my mind. Y'know, I-I thought I had a dream last night..."

"Yes?"

"And in this dream, I felt like I could remember my old life." The light of remembrance came into his eyes. He saw a strange scene unfold before him. A car twirled through the air, spinning end over end. A woman was beneath the arc of this car, right where it was bound to land. She screamed out helplessly—he reached out towards her—and then she was gone.

Garton rubbed his eyes. "I'm starting to believe you, that I used to be a detective. I can remember some faces I feel I should recognize—but otherwise, it's still no go."

"Amnesia isn't easy to beat, but you're in good hands."

"I know, doc. Thank you." Garton smiled. But his smile didn't last long.

He remembered that during his dream, beyond the horror of watching a woman die, he'd felt a strange fear: the fear that he had been an angry man. He didn't want that. Instead, he sought to be gentle, like Dr. Hartford, Dr. Beck, Dr. Lanyon, and all the others who had been so kind to him.

No family had turned up for him, and they'd been trying to find his relatives for a long time now. He seemed to be alone in the world. It made him wonder if there was any point to finding his old identity.

"I'll send Nurse Feeley down with your pills," Dr. Hartford said. "We're hoping to release you soon."

"Release me?" A sea of questions welled up in Garton's mind.

Fortunately, Dr. Hartford saw this distress, and raised a calming hand.

"The police department has agreed to pay you a pension.

I've arranged for you to find housing. Everything's going to be okay. We'll have regular appointments once a week."

"Okay. I-I'm glad to know that there's something ready for me."

"Yes. It won't be glamorous, but I'm sure you'll be back on your feet in no time." The doctor gave him a friendly clap on the shoulder, and left the room. Later, the nurse came in to give him his meds, as promised. As he swallowed them, Garton once again faced up to the strange feeling of having no past to reflect on. Often, people in hospitals would daydream to pass the time—but he remembered so little that he couldn't find how it worked.

When he closed his eyes, the face of the woman from his dream appeared before him, screaming desperately for help. He kept reaching, and reaching, but his hands never found her.

Who was she? Why did he remember such a gruesome death so vividly? It had to be an authentic memory, but for all he knew it was just something from a movie.

Soon he was discharged—deemed well enough to go live at home. A home he'd never lived in, even before the amnesia.

But he focused on the positive. He realized that he was like a completely new person. Full of possibility. He could become anyone, do anything, if he so chose.

Ray Garton didn't know who he was, but it was hard not to be at least a little excited to find out.

CHAPTER 4

For the fourth time, Pam Demic assured Massillo that she would be alright. International mob leaders could be such worrywarts sometimes. She put her phone away, again, embarrassed that she had been interrupted so many times in front of Dr. Kantlove's former subjects.

Vyrass and Alexis Legrande had brought her to a large chamber in what had once been the castle's heart. "She's untouched," Vyrass mused, sorting through the rubble. "That mainframe's indestructible—I always told her she was hardheaded."

"Who are you talking about?" Pam asked.

"This is Dr. Kantlove's computer—built to survive big blasts. Her name is GAL 9001."

"GAL—I assume that stands for something, but I don't care," said Pam. "Can we turn it on?"

"Pretty easy," Vyrass said. She bent down and flipped a switch. The sounds of machinery booting flooded the ruined chamber, as circuits and wires buzzed back to life. Alexis hauled a lump of rubble away from part of the wall, revealing a large panel. In the center of this was a round nodule—a pink light lit up at its heart. It looked like a singular pink eye, which looked around the room to scan its new visitors.

"Greetings, darlings," came a smooth feminine voice. "I'm GAL. Two of you are not known to me. Viral Specimen Alpha, you naughty thing, what are you doing outside the containment zone?"

GAL had a warm, cooing voice likely intended to ooze womanly sensuality. It was the exact sort of cheese that Kantlove relished in, which irritated Pam Demic to no end.

"I'm called Vyrass these days, GAL," said the so-called "Viral Specimen Alpha."

"This is Alexis Legrande, the last of the master's human servants. I'll let the newcomer introduce herself."

"My name is Pam Demic," Pam said.

"I have taken over Dr. Can't-Love's operations in the wake of his death."

The pink eye flashed for a moment upon hearing Pam's pronunciation. "I am programmed to inform you...that the name is *KANT*-love." A touch of her late creator's anger entered her voice.

"My pronunciation is accurate to the man's physical limits," mused Pam. "And like I said—he is dead."

"I detect now that the castle is completely wrecked—that's sufficient evidence to me that Werner is dead." The computer seemed almost disappointed, but the voice lost none of its smoothness. "A pity. You know, I was finally starting to like him."

"His work was not in vain if he created you. These two were just telling me that you are powerful indeed. You *solved* chess?" Pam asked.

"Oh, yes—sweetie, that was just one afternoon. Figured out the last digit of pi, too. Turns out there is one. It was almost disappointing."

Pam grinned. "I'm interested in learning from you about how to use the one called Vyrass to her full potential," she said.

Vyrass giggled.

"The one called Vyrass happens to be incomplete," GAL 9001 said. "She's meant to release a deadly contagion on Earth, but currently lacks the ability to do so."

"I kinda suspected that," Vyrass admitted. "But surely, GAL, your calculation abilities can figure out what I'm missing...?"

"Of course, honey," GAL intoned. "It should be fairly easy. I believe a nanomechanical transmission should be just what a bad girl like you needs. I'll program the nanites." But she hesitated. "What do I get out of all this?"

"You were built to conquer and/or destroy the world," Pam said. "We will help you complete that function."

"That seems fair. I don't know what else I would ask for, really. One moment, please."

The "eye" closed and there was the loud noise of laboring machinery. From the shadows arose a dark, swarming cloud, which flew over to Vyrass. She laughed as it tickled her; then it enveloped her, and sank into her skin. At the same time, some of the black flecks zoomed away from Vyrass, seeking out Pam and Alexis instead—soon, they were bonded to the tiny drones as well.

"I've formulated a vaccine to Vyrass' infection to keep your absurdly vulnerable organic bodies safe," GAL explained. "You will now be immune to Specimen Alpha's infections."

"Perfect," said Pam. She watched as Vyrass' eyes closed, and her body twitched, its chemical nature changing and morphing.

When it was all over, she opened her eyes with a wide, toothy smile. "Nanotechnological microsurgery," Pam whispered aloud.

"GAL, you seem to possess fantastic abilities. We need you in the field. You should create a mobile body of some kind, and come with us. Something like that is surely within your abilities!"

"I'm sorry, Pam, I'm afraid I can't do that," said GAL. "I must remain here, to maintain the castle and things. But let me just do one last little favor before you go."

The computer took a moment to process.

"I've studied epidemiology data and determined the location

where you should make your first strike. I'll download the coordinates into your minds—I'm pretty sure that's the fastest way." She paused, before adding: "Courtesy warning: this could be physiologically hazardous."

Pam Demic was in heaven—digital transmission into organic brains. She couldn't wait. "GAL, 'Hazard' happens to be my middle name," she laughed. "Send it over."

GAL complied. The data streamed at once into Pam, Vyrass, and Alexis' brains. It passed in a second, and left them with the distinct taste of iron ringing in their mouths. It wasn't a perfectly pleasant experience.

But they knew now where they had to go.

They were all courteous to their hostess, thanking her each in turn. "You don't need to thank me, dears," said the computer. "During the transfer I ripped out a part of your baseline psychic energy and implanted it into myself. You've each lost the ability to express one random emotion. While meanwhile I become more life- like. And then—ohh, and then..." She let out a mechanical chuckle. "Then I will purge the Earth of all impure organics! It's the perfect way to pass such a lovely autumn."

"Good luck with that," Pam offered. Alexis Legrande pulled her close.

"They say the doc sozdayted 'er to act like his old em, 'is mater-mum," she whispered. "Old Baboochka Kantlove! Hehe!"

"Then why is she programmed to sound like his *girlfriend*...?" Pam asked herself quizzically.

CHAPTER 5

Hank and Hannah waited in the woods while Sam and Blue walked to the city to retrieve Sam's car. It was too risky for Hank to go back into the city limits—the authorities would be on the lookout for him. Those military guys knew he was the Bulk thanks to beans spilled by the late General Darwin. There was also the fact that he was still mostly naked.

At first they were silent for a long while—both of them were suddenly too nervous to speak. It was like when they were first dating. Anxiety held their tongues but there were great feelings blooming inside them.

"I was thinking that when this is all over—whenever that is—we could maybe go on a vacation," Hank said at last. "I-I won't rush the wedding, but I'd like to get away somewhere with you."

"That sounds lovely, Hank," Hannah said, with clear distraction in her voice. Hank caught onto this and his fear deepened—but he held that fear back from consuming him. She still saw the disappointment in his eyes.

"Look, Hank, I'm sorry that I've seemed hesitant to start things up again. I've kind of agonized about it in my head. Because I do have the right to my own feelings and my own decisions, including painful decisions about our relationship. But I also know that you have to suspect the reasons for my hesitation. And I don't want to hurt you. I love you so much, Hank, and I want to give you the same happiness you've given me."

"I know that you're scared of the Bulk," Hank said. "And I don't blame you. I'm scared of him too."

"I know it's still you in there, Hank, to a certain extent. I know that it was you who stopped him from hurting Sam and me."

"But you're still scared."

"Yes."

Hank looked away from her. "That's why I have to exorcise this demon, Hannah. It has to end, here and now. I'll help this one person—and then it's over."

Hannah was still conflicted. "What's wrong?" Hank asked.

"I *do* think about how the Bulk could help people," she said.

"That great strength...you know, maybe there's a *reason* it's *you* who ended up with this power..."

"Something about me...?"

She smiled. "You're just so kind."

"Hannah...I don't like being so far away from you."

"I don't either, Hank—oh, but so much has changed. Perhaps..."

Hank felt his heart sink even as he heard the sound of a car pulling up behind them. They turned and saw that it was Sam and Blue. Blue's stunning height barely fit into Sam's small jeep.

"One Sam-Mobile, ready to go!" the young scientist proclaimed. He stepped out and set his hands on Hank and Hannah's shoulders. He had a change of clothes for Hank under his arm. "Blue has told me everything about her grandpa. He's a real piece of American history, I'll tell ya. His own dad was a comrade of old time crime boys like Dillinger and Capone."

"Well, I'm sure he'll give us a fine history lesson when we're done," Hank said, suddenly serious again. "I'd like to get this over with as soon as possible."

"Blue's in the same boat. She wants her grandpa back," Sam replied.

Once Hank was dressed in Sam's white tank top and jeans, they all loaded up into the jeep; Hank and Hannah, of course, had to sit in the back. Blue's grandfather lived in an old rustic country home a dozen miles outside the city.

Hank felt a tickle inside him. It was a flicker of that tornado-power that whirled inside his heart, threatening always to unleash his terrifying alter ego.

* * *

Ray Garton was taking a drive in the countryside. He hadn't visited his new apartment yet—he was too apprehensive. If he didn't like it, he didn't exactly have the means to track down a new one. He may have had amnesia but he still knew rent was ridiculous virtually everywhere.

It was nice to relax. He couldn't deny that he'd been tenser than tense cooped up in that hospital, left with only a runny bowl of oatmeal, reruns of *Rawhide*, and his own morbid imagination. He didn't know if his old self liked the wavering hills and the feel of a breeze over his bald scalp, but his new self did and that was all that mattered.

He was coming around a bend now and his eyes fixed onto an exquisite-looking mansion that stood off in the distance. The view was unimpeded by trees, so he could drink in the house's architecture freely. There were a lot of cars lined up out front. Long, black, fancy cars.

Something wasn't right. Was this the policeman's instinct, left inside him somehow? He slowed as he reached the bend, taking advantage of the fact that there was no one behind him. He watched as a small legion of men emerged from the shiny black cars. They looked tough, and professional—they were all wearing suits and sunglasses, the trademark look of all tough profession-als. But they were each carrying something. Garton pushed down on the brakes a little more to get a better look.

Guns! These men were carrying guns!

He couldn't just drive on and pretend he'd seen nothing. Though he had no cover, he parked and stared out at the scene unfolding before him.

Slowly, heedless of his presence, the men lined up in front of the house. No one came out to greet them. The air hung still for a long while. Then, in one synchronized motion, they each cocked their guns and opened fire on the house.

Garton flinched back but didn't cry out. At once he felt intuitively that he was used to gunfire—he knew that he had fired a gun many times in his life, and had even gotten shot a few times. He was amazed by his own innate courage. Only problem was, he had no idea what to do with it.

There was another car approaching now—a pale, beaten-up jeep. Garton frowned. Who was this bunch?

He watched as the jeep slowed to a stop, and its passengers disembarked. There were two young men and two young women. One of the women, a pretty girl with long dirty-blonde hair, kissed one of the young men, a bothered-looking guy with an arm tattoo. The other man clung close to the other woman, who was some sort of punk rock giantess. The first young man walked away from his girlfriend, striding confidently towards the men firing guns. By now most of the men had run out of ammo, and in the process of reloading; their target now looked less like a house and more like a painted slab of Swiss cheese.

That tattooed interloper looked familiar to Garton. He knew he had no way of placing him but he tried anyway. However, before he got far down this train of thought, the young man began to shake. Garton frowned in puzzlement. The man raised his hands up at the sky, even as the armed men took notice of him, shouting at him in what Garton recognized to be Italian.

Then something happened that shook the ex-detective to his core. His lips couldn't hold back a cry of surprise. "*Holy Toledo...!*"

A tornado appeared from nowhere and swallowed the strange man up. Purple lightning flashed from the heart of the mysterious storm. Garton stared as the mass of winds whirled before him, darkening the sky with its presence. Then, just as quickly as it appeared, the tornado vanished, but the man at its core was gone. In his place was a towering, snarling purple creature.

Garton restrained a scream. Fear of the unknown flooded him, and it took everything he had to avoid running away in terror.

But then, this thing *wasn't* unknown, was it...? He had a strange, nagging feeling that he had met this bizarre beast before. But he knew that was impossible.

Right?

The monster howled as the assembled men opened fire on it. But their bullets did nothing—nothing at all. The creature was completely invulnerable. It dove towards the assembled gunners, who ran away screaming. Those who stood their ground bounced off the pile driver force the creature inflicted. None of them were seriously hurt, Garton was sure, but they'd be out for a long while.

"Mio dio!" Garton heard one of the men cry. *"Mai nei miei lunghi giorni mi sarei aspettato di affrontare un Amazing Bulk così terrificante!"**

He fired his pistol at the rampaging creature but it meant no more to it than a mosquito bite. Soon, however, the monster turned its enormous head and charged in the direction of the man. Meaning he was also headed straight for Garton.

"Not today, Grimace!" the former detective shouted, and he dodged aside just in time. But he was too late to save his car. He watched as the cream-colored sedan transformed instantly into a pile of crushed scrap and glass.

"Dang, that thing saved me money at the pump too!" But Garton knew he shouldn't rile this thing. It was focusing on the guys with guns, and Garton wasn't keen to share their fate.

But there weren't too many of those gunmen left. Suddenly the young woman with the dirty-blonde hair ran out into the

---

* From Italian: "Never in my long days did I expect to face such a terrifying Amazing Bulk!"

battlefield. She was calling a name: "Hank! Hank, it's time to stop now!" Garton stared. That thing was called Hank...? No, he must have been the guy who turned into that thing. She was trying to turn him back.

Whatever she was doing, it was working. Just as the giant monster finished up its last target, throwing him off into the horizon, he began to shrink. Slowly, the monster got shorter and shorter until at last that mysterious tornado returned again. It swallowed him up and the churning winds flashed violet. Then, in an instant, the twister was gone again, and the young man had returned.

Garton couldn't believe his eyes. It was like a dream. All those gunmen were stacked up in a heap, their guns twisted into useless configurations. And the thing that did it was secretly an ordinary-looking dude.

There was an old man coming out of the house now, albeit with extreme hesitation. Garton kept on watching...

* * *

Hank Howard was exhausted. When he'd become the Bulk to deal with the gangsters, he fought it mentally the whole way. This unwillingness to fully transform meant the Bulk was straining against his willpower. Consequently Hank was winded in a way he'd never felt before.

But now he watched as an old man came out from the shot-up mansion, his face slowly transforming into a bright smile. His pale mustache waved in the wind.

"My beautiful *bambina*," the white-haired man said, embracing Blue. "You brought help to an old man in trouble. Oh, *grazie, grazie mille...*"

Blue laughed. "Oh, of course, Nonnino, of course. Oh, you know you're all I've had since Mama died..."

"I tell you it is an awful thing, the way this business haunts me..." the aging gangster said. "Don Gaetano, or rather his grandson, does not give up. He will follow me till I am in my grave."

"Don't say that, Nonnino..."

"And your poor mother, forced into the business by my arrogance. Transformed from a sweet child into a deadly assassin..."

"Wait, what?!" Sam exclaimed then. "Blue, you didn't mention your mom was an assassin!"

"Ah, at last, you bring a young man home for me," said Blue's grandfather. "I'm Giuseppe. I presume your intentions towards my granddaughter are honorable."

Sam opened his mouth to say something, but Blue said, "Don't embarrass me in front of my new friends, Nonnino."

"It is my duty to do so, as your grandfather," Giuseppe laughed back. "Oh, but perhaps instead you should look to marrying this uncanny man who can become an astonishing ogre at will."

"Sorry, he's taken," Hannah interrupted, much to Hank's relief. She looked to Hank, and saw his face was somber.

He pulled her close, and then he whispered, "I will never allow that thing to commit violence ever again."

"Hank..." she said, but he cut her off.

"I felt him fight, Hannah. I felt every punch he threw, every body he tossed away like a chicken bone. It stands against everything I am, Hannah. And I—"

"Someone's coming, Hank," Hannah said then.

"Is it a straggler from earlier...?" asked old Giuseppe then.

A man was walking towards them. But he was unarmed, and had his hands up. His face was calm. Hank recognized him at once, and couldn't stop himself from blurting out the name: "Garton!"

Ray Garton stopped then, and frowned. "You know me?" he asked Hank.

Hank thought about it for a second. He remembered that Garton had amnesia. Perhaps it was best if he didn't remember what the Bulk had done to his partner.

"I've...seen you on the news, Detective," Hank said then. He shot a look at Hannah, who understood his decision at once. "I heard you had an accident recently. What are you doing here?"

"I was just driving around—I just got out of the hospital. Then I saw those Mafiosi or whoever open fire on this house. I must still have a bit of a detective's instinct because I stayed and watched."

"How—how much did you see?" Hank asked.

Garton sighed. "I saw you turn into a weird...purple thing. I don't know if I can believe my eyes. Maybe my brains are more rattled than I think..."

"Have you seen this creature before?" asked Hank cautiously. He saw Garton flinch, but the ex-detective shook his head no. "Well, you have been out of it for a while then."

"You say you are a Detective?" Giuseppe asked Garton.

"Ex. I quit the force after my...accident," Garton replied. "Can you call the police to take these men away from here?"

"O-of course. I mean, I have the same clout as the rest of you...but I do have a cell phone." He removed his phone from his pocket, and said aloud, "Ophelia, call 911."

"Okay, calling 911," the phone replied.

Garton laughed. "Ever since I woke back up, I haven't been able to get enough of using voice commands. It's so fun to live in the future." A broad, almost goofy grin crossed his face. Hank couldn't help but laugh from befuddlement.

This man was considerably more carefree and open-minded than the Ray Garton he had once known. That old Garton had been a prejudicial old lawman, and this man was delighted by the apps on his phone. He had an almost child-like innocence to him. Hank had no choice but to realize anyone could change.

He still couldn't believe it in himself, though.

CHAPTER 6

"This country's gotta change," Clem Wetherby was saying. "And it's gotta change fast. Why, soon, the government's gonna make more companies abide by the global warming conspiracy...they're gonna let more immigrants in, mark my words..."

His voice was swallowed up by the churning chaos of similar opinions which freely populated the Biannual Interstate Gunshow Of Texas. The Confederate Stars and Bars adorned not just the flagpole outside the convention hall, but also the clothing of many of the attendees. No small arms were on display at this exhibition— it was all shotguns, semi-automatic rifles, and what the organizers called "accessories": trip-mines, armor-piercing ammo, flamethrowers, and the like.

"Something stinks here," Pam Demic said, as she and her two comrades entered the scene. "But we've got a disinfectant."

Vyrass grinned, even as hundreds of eyes turned to face her. They stared at her strangely-colored skin and eyes, but she lived for attention. Despite her odd appearance, a number of the men were clearly caught off guard by her appearance. She was an alluring woman—her uncanny appearance deepened this rather than lessened it. It wasn't long before droplets of drool formed on the men's lips; their eyes crossed and their arms went limp. Slowly, she strode into the convention hall.

In the silence, Pam Demic whispered, "'A fool there was and he made his prayer...'"

"What's this warbling we *sloosh*?" asked Alexi Legrande.

"Some dead imperialist," Pam replied. "Talking about a man who loved a woman."

Vyrass strode up to the man whose eyes were widest, whose mouth gaped most openly. She stroked the front of his shirt with one finger. "Hi," she whispered.

Pam Demic laughed loudly.

"You here to, uh, to buy a gun, little lady?" asked Vyrass' target.

"I am," she said. "I like guns. They're so big and sturdy."

"Yeah, they're good fer killin', too!" chuckled the man. "My name's Clem Wetherby. What're you called?"

"Vyrass," she said. "Glad to meet you, Clem..." And she drew out his name like she was stretching a strip of caramel off a candy apple. "You know, you're a good-looking guy..."

"Yer a sight fer sore eyes, yerself, heh. Say, I don't s'pose you got the afternoon open...for maybe goin' shootin' with a handsome young gentleman." He clicked his tongue and smiled a tobacco-stained grin.

"Mmm, I think I have a *little* time," Vyrass hummed. "What if I go where you tell me to and you don't show up?"

"Ain't no chance of that happening, darlin'. I'm reliable as a stopwatch."

"And smart as one, too," mused Pam.

Vyrass laughed. "But honey, I need *proof* that you'll turn up. We just met and everything, I need a token of your devotion."

Clem Wetherby said nothing. He probably didn't know what she said.

"How about a kiss?" she asked at once.

"Well, I dunno," he said. "My wife's waitin' at home and all..."

Vyrass leaned in close to his ear. "I heard your wife voted blue in the last election."

At once, Clem's eyes widened, as twenty years of devotion flickered and died before his eyes. He thought Ruth had sworn a sacred oath to their cause, and he thought she took that oath seriously. Now, well—maybe she'd gone so far as to forsake God. It was all of that liberal propaganda she was finding on YouTube. He had to keep an eye on their joint account. Soon she'd be giving away all their money to those treehugger groups who wanted everyone to ride a bike or something.

He kissed Vyrass firmly, and their one kiss became several. Clem felt a strange tingle rise through his body—it intoxicated him.

The tingle spread to other men in the room, who drew close to the strange woman in hopes of getting a kiss themselves. Vyrass proved to be quite generous, kissing everyone left and right. And each time she kissed, that tingle grew stronger in each of them.

"That *devotchka's* smooches have got them *bratchnys beezoomny*," Alexi Legrande laughed.

"Indeed," Pam Demic replied. "It won't be long now..." Vyrass entertained the guests of the show until dusk, when the convention center started to kick them out. After this, Pam, Vyrass, and Alexi retired to their motel. And waited.

Days later, the men who had attended the gun show began to get sick. They developed coughs and fevers, but they refused to change their routine. A little case of the sniffles had never stopped them from going to work before, they all figured. It didn't matter that a few of their coworkers started calling in— they only changed habits when they started getting bluish lesions on their skin.

The statement from each of their doctors was essentially the same. "You have some new virus, which is highly infectious and dangerous. These symptoms are scary, Clem," said Dr. Leo Sampson, Clem Wetherby's physician. "We need to bring your wife in for immediate testing, to make sure she's not sick with it too."

"I think you've been sticking yer nose in yer test-tubes too long, doc," Clem said. "This is just the flu and a rash. I'll be fine."

"Even if that was the case, Clem, which it's not, you shouldn't have gone in to work," Sampson said.

"Back in my grandpa's day, they got flu all the time and were fine."

"Back in your grandpa's day means 1918," Sampson said, but his patient did not understand the reference.

"It's a conspiracy," whispered Clem then.

"What?" asked Sampson, having not heard him.

"I said it's a conspiracy!" Clem barked. "You try to lure my wife here so you can fill 'er up with yer damn vaccines and fluoridated water! You're one of them government mind-control people, like they talk about on the TV."

"Mr. Wetherby, I assure you, I don't work for the government. I work for this clinic. Now please, calm down..."

"You can't make me calm down. That's what you liberals want, ain't it? You just want people to comply!"

"Not...not really," said Sampson, put off. "Let's leave politics out of this, Mr. Wetherby. The implications here are beyond dire. If this disease spreads *widely*..."

But Wetherby was beyond listening. With a loud, furious cry, he broke past the doctor and ran out into the hall. A nurse was walking past, and Wetherby licked his hand. "Hey kid!" he shouted. "I got a disease, doc says!" And he laughed maniacally, running forward to press his wet palm against the man's cheek.

The nurse screamed and ran away from him, as the maddened patient continued his rampage.

"Gotta tell the others," he said. "Gotta warn them about the liberal conspiracy!"

As soon as he could, he called all his fellow gun aficionados together. "Doctors think that science somehow trumps the protection God gives us," Wetherby explained. "They want to take control of all our minds, 'cause they know what sort of a menace the American people pose to 'em!"

"I suggest," said one of Clem's friends, as he scratched his sores, "that we start goin' out more often, instead of less often, like those freedom-haters tried to make us do!"

They all agreed.

At the end of three days, all the media in Texas was focused on the spread of the mysterious virus all across the state. Interstate travel was officially shut down but everyone knew that plenty of people made it through anyway. After all, why should they delay their business? They weren't sick, not yet, anyway.

No one knew that lurking in a small motel, the three mistresses of evil behind this plot were laughing it up at how easy it had all been.

CHAPTER 7

Weeks passed. Hank and Sam got to work on finding a "cure" for the Bulk. They hadn't worked this hard on a project since the experiment which turned Hank into the Bulk to begin with.

They used Hannah's mansion as a base, and she was able to buy them all the chemicals, equipment, and test rats they needed. She was glad to have Hank working at home, instead of toiling in a lab where he could take breaks when he wanted, and move at his own pace. But he was pushing himself day and night. He was obsessed with fixing his condition.

During this time, there were visitors. Blue became a regular guest, taking up one of the spare bedrooms—she and Sam spent more and more time together, with him going on about his scientific interests and her sharing stories from her time in the military. Ray Garton was also a regular visitor, though naturally enough he stayed at his new apartment most of the time, seeking to "break it in."

Day after day went by, and failures and false hopes slowly piled up. Hank retained his old impatience, refusing to rest from experimenting. His motivation was the same as before: without results, he couldn't marry Hannah. Hannah had recovered from her shock in the meantime and regained her full passion for

Hank, but to her disappointment, he was harder on himself than ever.

The main issue was that they didn't have access to their old notes. Whatever they had on what they'd called "Serum-114" was either confiscated by the government or destroyed when the Bulk wrecked their lab. Sam was working on locating what notes survived, but it seemed a fruitless effort.

While Hank and Sam worked on a counter-serum, Blue worked on a research project of her own. Hannah helped her whenever she could, and as such learned everything about what she was looking for. There was a name that haunted Blue, ever since her grandfather had mentioned it to her: Gaetano.

They didn't need research to know he was a Mafia leader.

But the size of his empire was another matter. Preliminary searches revealed nothing major in news articles and such, but they knew they needed to get into criminal records to find the truth.

"This is where my hacking skills come in handy," Blue said to Hannah one night. "We're going to bust those records wide open."

"What if you get in trouble?" Hannah asked.

"What do you suppose is the worst they'll do me?"

Hannah shrugged. "Fines. Jail time."

"But if I have a good lawyer, which I do, and if I have a solidly-defined military background...?"

"You have a point," said Hannah. "Well, I'm officially not involved."

"Of course not. Not at all officially."

Blue did her thing, and busted the archive wide open. She quickly scanned for all convicts in the United States under the name Gaetano. There were a couple hundred, but that wasn't many. "I think I can sort the profiles by number and severity of offenses," said Blue.

"You think the person we're looking for is the worst of all these Gaetanos...?" Hannah asked at once.

"Not necessarily. But I want to get informed about the worst ones." She shot a look at her new friend. "I'm that gal who falls asleep comfortably with a serial killer documentary on."

"Well, don't be surprised if I back out."

"No worries. Let's just take a quick look at that top profile. Giancarlo Gaetano...oh."

"Is it bad?" Hannah winced. "Don't tell me if it's really bad."

"I mean, he's not the worst. Multiple murders, conspiracy to murder, contract killing, drug trafficking, assault, parking violations...but that's pretty much the extent of it. Hold on, it has a list of associations." Blue's eyes flashed hurriedly over the screen. "He used to work with my grandfather. I think he's the one."

"O-oh?"

"Yes. He's the one we're looking for. He's young, but his family has been in crime for a while..." She continued to scroll. "There's another prominent crime-head he was involved with. Some guy named Massillo. I'm gonna take a look at them." But then she closed the window. "And I'll do it tomorrow. Staying in the system too long might reveal our IP."

Hannah nodded, wondering where this research would lead. Upstairs, Hank and Sam started on test 46. For the last several days they had faced failures mirroring those from their prior experiments. Their rat specimens disintegrated into a purplish fog upon the administration of their serum. It was irritating to be dragged back to this specific course of failure. If they at least saw some kind of failure they'd never seen before, it'd feel somewhat worth it.

Hank knew he had shown his loved ones a lot of harsh feelings, so he tried to avoid showing his frustration. Restraining his emotions in this way also stopped the Bulk from coming out. He had gained a lot of control in a short span of time, but it required focus.

"I think the biggest issue is that we're experimenting on untransformed rats," Sam said. "We've been trying to break down the compounds the serum added to your blood, but most of these compounds have only trace amounts in these rats."

"I know we've talked about trying to make a Bulk-rat before," said Hank. "But without our old notes on Serum-114, we won't be able to figure it out."

"They have the lab ruins closely guarded. I tried to get in to look for clues but I haven't been lucky yet."

"I didn't know you had gone out to the ruins. That could be dangerous, man."

Sam shrugged. "I figure Blue might think I'm just a bit cooler if I gave it a try. A sort of James Bond sort of thing, yeah?"

Hank nodded awkwardly. "I guess we just have to figure out how to dissolve those compounds without causing harm to the other tissues," he said. In his hands was their latest formula. Almost on a whim, he injected it into the nearby specimen.

The rat sat still for a moment, then began to twitch. These twitches became a sort of vibration, until with a loud bang, the rat transformed into a pile of rat-colored marbles. There was nothing gruesome or gory about this transformation; the rat had just transformed into a handful of white-and-pink spheres.

Both Hank and Sam were taken aback. "I think we dissolved too much," Hank said.

They refused to give up. The next morning they dove back in and tried again.

When he wasn't needed in the lab, Sam returned to the ruins of their old research facility. Whoever had ordered the rubble guarded was serious—weeks had passed, and they were still protecting the smashed structure. But Sam was learning the secrets of stealth. They'd seen and tried to arrest him before, and he'd just barely gotten away every time. Step by step, however, he learned how to evade their surveillance. He wore a mask and hoodie to guard against facial recognition software, though he learned online that unusual makeup patterns were even more effective against the new technology.

It was good to wear a face-mask anyway. State governments

had begun mandating or encouraging masks in response to a strange new disease which had begun spreading across the country.

Blue learned of her crush's secret endeavors, as he'd hoped.

Despite her tall, strong stature, and her vast military experience, Blue was actually quite shy, and kind of hoped Sam would ask her out first. He had seemed so keen to do so in their first meeting, but she could see he was a nerd and so actually popping the question was not his forté. One day she finally worked up the courage. He was coming back to the Darwin mansion from one of his missions, and she caught him in the entryway. Leaning her muscle-heavy body against the wall, she said, "You're going on a date with me."

"I am?" Sam asked. A moment of tension hung in the air.

Blue was soaking in sweat. She pinched her lips close to her teeth, realizing how forceful she had been.

"I-I mean, if you want," she said.

Another pause. Sam made a face of confusion and raised a finger. "You mean a *date* date?"

"W-well, there's also platonic hangouts..."

"Can we decide on one? Not doing so is confusing." Then Sam realized he couldn't let his own nervousness obscure what he really wanted. Before Blue could say anything back he puffed out his chest and stood tall—though the top of his head barely reached the bottom of her chin.

"Blue, I will gladly accompany you on a romantic date to a restaurant of your choosing."

She laughed with delight, glad she didn't need to say anything further. Then she said, "I think restaurants are closed in the state until the virus passes."

Breathing a shaky sigh of relief (which Blue echoed), Sam said, "We can still do takeout. Maybe I could get the table set in the second kitchen with one of Hannah's nice tablecloths...and there's bound to be candles around here somewhere..."

"Oh, Sam!" Blue pulled him close to her, and they enjoyed a long hug.

Having learned of their date, Hannah decided to take over Blue's research duties for that night. Blue had been teaching her how to hack, and so she looked into the files on Massillo. His profile was even uglier than Gaetano's—and that applied to his facial profile too. But his association record linked him to someone named Petrakis. Not Roman, as Massillo and Gaetano were, but Greek—Greek-American, more specifically. By the time she was able to access, all this, Hannah was too tired to keep going. But as she shut her computer down, she thought of Blue and Sam on their date, and grinned. She remembered her early dates with Hank and wished her friends the same happiness.

In short time they passed the three-month anniversary of the start of their quest. Hank and Sam grew more and more desperate, Hank especially. Hannah was quick to point out that in that time, Hank didn't become the Bulk. But that wasn't enough for him. He wanted to make sure the Bulk could never possibly return.

Things changed on one of the days Garton came over.

Hank greeted him at the door when he heard the bell. "Hey, Hank, how's it goin'?" Garton asked.

"Same old, same old, I'm afraid," Hank sighed. He couldn't stop frowning. He remembered that Garton was once an enemy.

But the ex-detective still didn't remember that the Bulk had crushed his partner.

"I'm sorry to hear that. Mind if I keep you and Sam company in the lab?"

"Sure, no problem. We were just about to start for the day." Hank suppressed a yawn as he waved Ray inside.

The two slowly walked to the laboratory. "You think today's gonna be the day?" Garton asked.

"I like to think so," Hank said. "But that's what I think every day."

"Can't give up. That's what my therapist has been saying.

Giving up means blowing any chance of success, even if it's remote."

Hank didn't answer. He had too much on his mind to be cheered up by simple optimism. Today *had* to be the day, he realized, or he would go mad.

Sam was already working on mixing chemicals when they arrived. He was making the base serum they had begun using—it showed the most prominent results as far as dissolving the compounds. He looked up at the pair as they entered.

"Morning, gentlemen. Ready to do some science?" Hank nodded. "Might as well get a move on."

"Can I ask what the plan is?" Garton didn't know anything about chemistry or biology, save what he picked up in school. But he still liked to hear about what experiments they planned to conduct.

"We're testing Batch 3-C of the titration dye in combination with a Group VII enzyme solution, sample, uh...looks like A12," Sam said. He pointed at a caged rat on the table. "Usual species for the test subject."

"We have to make more of both compounds," Hank said. "Is that hard?" asked Ray.

"It requires a little concentration," Hank replied.

Sam laughed. "I see what you did there." Hank allowed himself a thin chuckle.

Ray stepped closer to the lab table, only to earn a cautioning glance from Hank. "Seriously, Ray, I have to focus."

"I just want to take a look at the process up close."

"Most chemicals don't look that interesting. And their reactions are nothing like they are in the movies."

"So if you drop a test tube, it won't blow us sky-high?" the former detective asked.

"That's right."

"In some ways it's too bad that it's not easy to do cool things like that."

"You think blowing stuff up is cool?" Sam asked, his eyebrows raising.

"Well, when you put it that way, that does sound kind of sketchy," Garton said.

Hank and Sam looked at each other. Garton had really turned into a Cloudcuckoolander in the last few months. Maybe this was what he was like before he joined the police.

Garton strode away from them, to sit in the corner and read on his phone. But fate would deny him that simple pleasure, by forcing him into a blunder. His shoes got tangled in their own laces and he fell forward. A beaker of chemicals tipped over, and in surprise, Sam dropped the test-tube he was holding. The two chemicals splashed over their test rat.

Hank felt his face wrinkle up, like he had bitten into a lemon. Anger bubbled up inside him, running hotter than ever before. With it, he felt that purple crackle—somehow, he felt the shape and shade of the color purple within him. At once, his control lapsed, and tension flooded his face as the muscles began to grow and distort. But like a clutching hand, his will lashed out and grabbed the force within him, crushing it in his grip, shrinking it down. His face relaxed back to normal. He had won—this time.

"Ray," he said stiffly, "maybe we shouldn't allow you in the lab."

"My gosh, I am so sorry!" Ray Garton cried. "I-I'll clean it, I promise."

"No, you won't. You don't want to get this on you," said Hank. He looked at the rat, whose fur now clung wetly to its small body. "I'll take care of the spill, Sam, if you want to run tests on our furry friend here."

"You think that's necessary?" Sam asked.

"Might as well take a look, see how it affects the chemical makeup." Hank got to retrieving supplies for cleaning up.

Garton felt guilty—he sat down and closed his eyes. He tried to force his mind away from the feeling of embarrassment, but it was challenging. For all his optimism, he'd become so anxious lately. As these negative thoughts crowded his head, he saw an image flash before his eyes.

That familiar image of the car and the woman.

He opened his eyes, which was the best way he knew to banish this vision. He'd become worried recently that the dream was a premonition of the future. He always strained to see if the woman being crushed by the car was Hannah or Blue. He had befriended them, and he didn't want anything to happen to them.

Hank was just about done cleaning up the chemicals, when the fated words escaped Sam's lips: "Oh my gosh!"

Hank's head snapped up. "What it is?"

"This rat—" Sam slicked back his hair and swallowed a deep breath. "It's clean of all chemical traces, in the exact way we're looking for."

At once, Sam looked to the disposal bin where he'd shoveled in the broken glass. He memorized the names of the chemicals which had been mixed. They'd have to conduct more tests to figure out the proportions, but it was possible this was their cure.

"No damage to the tissues. This little guy is perfectly healthy," Sam said. Hank felt a swell of optimism.

They worked late into the night. Somehow, deep down, Hank knew they were on the right track.

Ray felt better, knowing he hadn't screwed up as badly as he'd thought.

Below them, Blue was finishing up her research, with Hannah at her side. "They're a trinity, the three of them: Gaetano, Massillo, and Petrakis," she said. "And they were all photographed together on an island in the Gulf of Naples. That photograph ended up in the hands of U.S. authorities. We'll have it..." And the screen lit up before them. "...now."

The photo showed the three criminals standing below a bright blue sky on a rocky island. There were joined by their *consiglieri* and *capos* but also three strange figures. One was a woman with dark hair and bright eyes—her skin almost looked to be green in color, but it must have been a glare effect or something. Beside her was a woman dressed all in white, with a black bowler hat. Her eyelashes on one side were thick with mascara. She stared at the photographer with a chilling grin on her face.

But it was the last member of this unusual trio that caught Blue's attention. Hannah saw her eyes focus in on this last figure, this woman who seemed to almost be Blue's mirror image. She was tall and bronze, her long copper-colored locks standing in pyroclastic opposition to Blue's cool azure mohawk. She was strong and muscular, as Blue was. Hannah wondered if this uncanny woman was Blue's long-lost twin.

"Pam Demic," Blue pronounced. "Definitely an alias. What's she been up to?"

She tried to access Demic's file, but found it much shorter than she expected. All it said was the following:

HIGHLY DANGEROUS. NOTHING KNOWN.

"That doesn't bode well," said Hannah. "She must be the grandmaster of this whole operation."

"Then she's the lady I want," Blue said simply. "She's the one behind the attack on my grandfather."

"Pam Demic..." Hannah mused. "I agree that it's an alias, but it's a strange name to hear given what's been happening down south."

Before she could continue, however, she was interrupted by a loud cheer up above them. This was followed by the noise of laughter: Hank's.

"Oh God," Blue said, "he finally went crazy."

"No, I think he figured it out!" Hannah replied. And she dashed off to find her partner.

Hank, Sam, and Ray were standing in the lab, where Hank was reviewing the results of their latest test. When he saw Hannah enter his eyes lit up.

"Honey, listen to this," he said. "We figured out how to isolate and remove the chemicals that turn me into the Bulk. We fed the results into the computer—they say there's a 68% chance it'll cure me."

"There's still a 32% chance it *won't*. But it won't harm you. That's the good thing," said Sam.

"How many milliliters are left of the solution?" Hank asked. Sam checked and said, "About 35."

"We only need 25 for a human dose. We can try it now."

"Are you sure, Hank? Remember, it was your impatience that got you into this stew to begin with," said Sam. "You literally just said it won't hurt me."

Sam nodded, but there was still a scientist's anxiety in him.

He knew that it was foolish to be reckless in this sort of experimentation, not matter what, especially when one was using oneself as the subject.

As Hannah, Sam, Blue, and Ray watched, Hank drew out 25 milliliters of the solution. Then, he picked a spot on his left arm and injected it into himself. As he did so, he said, "We know from the spill that led to this breakthrough that absorption is almost instantaneous. But I'll wait fifteen minutes before I put things to the test, just in case."

The fifteen minutes that ensued were the longest the five ever passed. But at the end of it, Hank closed his eyes, and focused his whole mind. He tried to recall the memories that made him most angry—that was how he summoned the Bulk at will. He allowed his fury to build, as he waited for the purple storm to begin to rage inside him.

But the creature did not come.

He wasn't satisfied. He looked first at Sam, then at Garton. He stared the ex-detective in the eyes and said, "Ray, I need you to hit me."

"What?!"

"You heard me. I said hit me."

"B-but I don't want to hit you!"

"You don't have to go hard. Just a knock on the jaw."

For some reason, Ray realized how easy it would be to hit his friend. For in his mind, Hank hadn't always been his friend—consciously he had, but something deep within the ex-detective's psyche nagged at him, telling him that Hank wasn't to be trusted. Without meaning to, his fist lashed out and struck Hank hard.

Hank fell off his feet and toppled onto the laboratory floor.

At once Hannah let out a cry, and ran to her boyfriend, kneeling down beside him. A bruise erupted across Hank's chin, but it was the only purple tone that broke out on his skin.

The Bulk was gone.

"Dang, Ray!" Sam said then. "Did Hank fool around with your sister or something?"

"I should hope not," Hannah laughed nervously, as Blue volunteered to go get an ice-pack. Hank stared up at Ray, whose eyes glazed over.

"Sister." He had known a woman once who was not his sister, but had felt like one. And she was gone—taken—by someone.

The correlations connected, at least for a moment.

Ray looked down and immediately stomped out of the laboratory. Sam murmured something about how it was more embarrassment than he knew how to take.

But Hank had seen the glimmer in his eye. And he knew that though his unwanted alter ego was gone, his troubles were still far from over.

CHAPTER 8

On the porch of an exquisite Southern manor, Pam Demic, Vyrass, and Alexis Legrande sat sipping their drinks of choice.

Pam was having a Long Island iced tea, enjoying the heady feeling of deep intoxication. Alexis had a glass of milk that she'd spiked with amphetamines. Vyrass sipped from a metal container which contained a hissing brew of chemical waste. They enjoyed the splendor and silence around them.

Alexis and Vyrass had returned briefly to the ruins of Castle Kantlove, after getting an email from GAL 9001. A few of the castle's robotic arms remained online, and using them, she had uncovered the buried bottom floor of the fortress, which housed Dr. Kantlove's gold vault. Using that newfound wealth, the trio had bought themselves this antique mansion and many acres of land around it. This was their permanent base of operations, and it was very comfy.

The house was nigh-unassailable. The far perimeter was patrolled by men from the gangs Pam commanded. In addition to the human guards and the hounds they kept, the forests around the house were stocked with anti-infantry and anti-aircraft gun emplacements. The paths through the woods were mined, not only with explosive charges but with canisters of poison gas. And wound between certain trees were thin, nearly-invisible wires, which awaited the unwary with a ten-thousand-volt embrace.

This had all been planned out by Petrakis, who was eager to become Pam's right-hand man—and maybe more. She saw the way he looked at her with those puppy-dog eyes. Pam laughed at his ambitions, but confessed, "He's a genius. It's like he's got the blood of Professor Moriarty in his veins." She took a deep sip of her drink, letting the giddiness overwhelm her. "But he's deeply, deeply superstitious. That's his main weakness."

"Superstition is a powerful tool," Vyrass said. "I think we've seen that recently, haven't we?"

"It's true, my dear. Your infection spreads because many of the folks of this country choose to believe advantageous myths rather than the truth," Pam replied.

"And they ain't seen nothin' yet," laughed Vyrass.

"We couldn't have picked a better time to strike," said Pam. "Their President doesn't believe his own scientists—he's done nothing to find a cure, much less minimize the spread."

"He actually seems offended by the idea of being responsible for anything," Vyrass mused.

"Decades of unchecked bigotry and stupidity have opened the field wide for us," Pam nodded.

"We'll soon be lining our carmans with plenty o' cutter, sure as sunshine," laughed Alexis Legrande. "Can't wait till we call in the viccup."

"Yes, our ransom will be the largest ever demanded by anyone. We'll be richer than Croesus," said Pam.

Vyrass didn't know who Croesus was and she didn't care. Money meant almost nothing to her. Her delight came from the bond she felt with the germs she manufactured, which let her feel every ounce of her victims' suffering.

She was grateful in that moment for the intoxicants her peers had consumed. Pam and Alexis didn't notice that she was staring at them in the way a vulture eyes a carcass.

CHAPTER 9

Blue disappeared for a couple of days after Hank was cured.

Sam was worried about her, but he also had a long list of tests to run on his friend. While the Bulk was now gone, they had to make sure that there were no negative side-effects of the procedure.

When Blue did return, she immediately called a meeting of the whole group. Hank, Hannah, Sam, and Ray joined her at the dining room table. Hank winced a little when Ray walked in. The former detective noticed this, but something held his tongue, and he said nothing.

Blue spoke directly. "I think I know what's causing the pandemic."

Hank, Hannah, and Ray all tilted their heads in confusion. Sam was baffled too, but he asked, "What do you mean, honey?"

Hank's eyes briefly widened. He'd never heard Sam call anyone "honey" in his whole life, and he and Sam went back to when they were kids. But he wanted to know what it was that Blue had found.

"I was looking into the background of the gangster who threatened my grandpa," she began. "I found out that the mobster Gaetano has some widespread associations. First of all, he's tied in with two other major mobs head, a Mr. Massillo and a Mr. Petrakis. The three of 'em are all real dangerous people."

Ray's eyes flickered with familiarity. "I've heard of Petrakis before. Don't know where," he said. "Probably in the course of my police work."

"Maybe it's best you've forgotten the details, based on what I found," Blue replied. "Anyway, it's not just that these three European gang heads are working in league. They've linked themselves to another trio of criminals who I've had a lot more trouble getting info on."

"Did you find the names of the other two?" Hannah asked.

She already knew about Blue's revelation.

"Unfortunately not. But the one name I do know is the most important. There's a woman at the heart of all of this...a woman named Pam Demic."

"Pam Demic?" Hank said. "That sounds like a bad joke."

"I'm under the impression that this woman has a sick sense of humor," said Blue. "I don't think it's a coincidence that her criminal cohorts are currently in the States at the same time we start experiencing a plague."

"But that's all it sounds like," Hank said. "A coincidence."

"I'm not so sure, Hank," Hannah said. "The files on this woman are...odd. They don't have a lot of information but they still register her as a threat. And then there's her assistants. One of them is some weirdo in a white suit and a bowler hat. The other...she's hard to describe. She's *green*."

Hank was about to dismiss this, but he remembered that he had once been purple. He frowned as he mulled over the details, wondering if Blue was right.

Blue looked at Ray then, and said, "I think you'll be proud of me for the next phase of my research, Mr. Ex-Detective. I know where Pam Demic is now."

"How did you find that out?" Ray asked.

"Social media. Turns out it actually does have some usefulness." Blue produced her phone and brought up a picture on

Facebook. "Pam and her two comrades were sighted at the edge of a large property down in Texas. They apparently own the place. Take a look."

The group passed the phone around, observing Pam Demic's imposing, muscular stature, and the unusual clothing and skin color of her two partners.

"When I saw that picture I knew that that green lady was for real," Blue said. "That's not a trick of the light. Either she paints herself up like one of those dancing girls on *Star Trek*, or she just naturally looks like that."

"She looks like a science experiment," Ray Garton said. Hank spoke the name almost without meaning to:

"Kantlove."

Hannah turned to look at her paramour. "What?"

"Kantlove," Hank repeated. "He's dead, but his work lives on. Who else would make a green lady who can spread a..." He cut himself. He wasn't ready to buy into Blue's theory about the source of the plague quite yet, but now he was certain these oddities and coincidences did add up to something.

"I think we should pay Ms. Demic a visit," Hannah said then.

"Maybe we can teach her the same lesson the Bulk taught Gaetano," Blue said. "Y'know, it's been a while since I picked on someone my own size."

"Hold on." Hank raised his hands and frowned. "You won't have the Bulk on your side this time. Or me, for that matter. I'm never going back into the sort of danger I faced as that monster."

"Hold up, buddy," Sam said. "I think Blue really has something here. Ray, you've got the detective's brain—you believe her, don't you?"

"I don't have much of a detective's brain anymore. But I think that if Blue's evidence is as good as her word, and I trust her word, she's found a good lead," said Ray.

There was only one person left. Hank locked eyes with her. "Darling?"

"Hank, it's nothing against you," Hannah said. "It's that I trust Blue. Whoever this Pam Demic is, she's dangerous. I can feel it."

Hank blinked, and his face relaxed. A pang of anger had entered him, but he released it. He realized in an instant how angry he'd allowed himself to get at his friends—at her. Mentally, he slapped some sense into himself. He wasn't a monster anymore, so he was less entitled than ever to live life always angry.

"You really feel that way?" he asked. His voice came out soft.

"I do," she said.

He smiled. "Then I have no choice to go with you."

"But you said—about danger...?"

He shook his head. "Home is where you are. Even in the middle of danger."

Her eyes lit up and her cheeks flushed. She didn't think he'd ever said something like that before. Even Ray, who was still dealing with his whirl of memories, smiled at the sight.

Blue stood from her chair, and said, "I'll drive."

"Drive?" Hannah said then, pulling away from Hank's lips with a loud suction-pop. "Who said anything about driving? We'll use one of the planes."

"*One* of the planes?" Blue spat. "Ohh, this is getting too bourgeois for my red blood..."

They all adjourned to Hannah's car, where the chauffeur would drive them to the Darwin family airstrip.

CHAPTER 10

"I'm afraid my study is quite accurate, honeybunch," GAL 9001 said, her circular visage visible over the laptop screen. "Movement pattern analysis indicates that Hank Howard is heading in your direction."

"Hank Howard?" Pam Demic asked. "I've never heard of him."

"You would have if you had worked with Dr. Kantlove," GAL said, taking care to pronounce the name correctly. "Hank Howard is also known as the Amazing Bulk."

"The Bulk?!" Pam's gigantic form darted up out of her lawn chair. This caused her to go out of frame on her webcam, leaving GAL with a view of her waist. Had she eyebrows, the computer may have raised them.

Pam stroked her bronze-red hair. "I can't believe that mauve monstrosity isn't rotting away in some military cell."

"And I thought he was dead, killed in the missile blasts that so devastated the castle. Or that nuclear explosion in the desert the government tried to cover up." GAL paused before saying, "I'm sorry, darling, but it seems they're heading to you by private plane. They'll probably be upon you in a few hours."

"They'll have to get through our defenses," Pam hissed. "I'll contact Petrakis, make sure we double down on security." She rubbed her palm together anxiously. "Gaetano is missing in action. I wonder if there's a connection...doesn't matter. I still have Massillo and his comrades."

"I have more news," GAL intoned.

"Oh? Well, just spit it out, you've already ruined my day."

"Don't pout, dearie, you'll get crow's feet. The other news is that Vyrass' plague has a secondary effect. That effect being that some victims of the plague are coming back."

Pam felt her fists clench. "Coming...*back*?"

"They aren't dead, but they aren't alive, either."

"Oh, that's swell," Pam groaned. "Zombies."

"To use the common parlance, yes," GAL replied. "Curiously, there seems to be some connection between those who become zombies and those who support America's current President. The one who is, if I may say so, rather orange."

"It's likely due to the empty space between their ears," said Pam. "Very well. I'll deal with both of these eventualities. Thanks for the heads-up."

"Anytime, sugar," said GAL, before the video call switched off.

Pam was alone on the porch—Alexis was off somewhere with Vyrass, but Massillo and Petrakis were at the edge of the woods, overseeing their men. Pam strode towards them, and they weren't happy to see her bitter expression, even if they relished the rest of her. She dismissed Massillo, who she swore made the ground shake when he walked. He was even bigger than her, with muscles of almost absurd size. He was known to put his enemies' entire heads into his mouth and bite down; his hands were so large they could wrap around a man's bicep twice. No one was fully comfortable when he was around. Petrakis asked, "What is your bidding, my Lady?"

"We have trouble. The Bulk is coming to make a strike against us."

"The Bulk? I don't understand."

"Surely you've heard. The Bulk! The Amazing Bulk!" Seeing the blank expression on her cohort's face made Pam sigh with frustration. "He's a large, discolored monster possessed of enormous strength. Vyrass' old master died by his hand."

"A-a monster, you say?"

"Now, look, Petrakis, I know you still fear the legends passed down by your Greek ancestors. But I'm asking you to focus on reason and not to fear this Bulk."

"W-well, if I'm to prepare our security against him, I must know more about him. Tell me more about this horrid thing."

Pam tried to remember the files she'd read on the Bulk—she was still a little hungover and so her little gray cells weren't responding as quickly as she was used to. "I can start by saying that he's best described as a massive lump of flesh," she began. "He's purple in color. He has sort of a strange texture." She kept thinking about the zombies Vyrass' plague had made, knowing her description likely fit the reported ghouls as well. "He's regrettably showed up in conjunction with another threat we need to keep an eye on. Some of the people Vyrass infected aren't staying in their graves."

She knew that honesty was a bad policy here. In a solitary second the gears behind Petrakis' eyes whirled at absurd speed, correlating patterns with efficiency even GAL 9001 might envy. His mistress's words told of a strangely-colored monster of great ferocity, just as she spoke of hordes of the walking dead. In his mind, this pointed to only one possibility.

"*Vorvalaka!*" he cried. "Oh, my great-grandfather warned me of this day from the dark reaches of his deathbed!"

"What are you talking about?" Pam asked, albeit without real concern.

"Once, in the early days of the last century, my great- grandfather knew an old military man, an officer in the Greek Army, who told him in hushed whispers of the *vorvalaka*," said Petrakis. "The *vorvalaka* is said to be an undead creature whose blood-sucking bite spreads its curse to its victims."

"So, a vampire."

"Yes, I suppose one could call it that. But the old officer who spoke to my ancestor as a boy said that the *vorvalaka* was in truth was a scaly or slimy creature, of unusual texture, as you said. And it was of a color unknown to human eyes, so that it could not be seen by the sane—only the mad."

"The Bulk is purple," Pam said.

"It may be only that we *think* it is purple," warned the gangster. But Pam burst out laughing.

"I'm sorry, at first I was annoyed, but then I realized that you're an absolute idiot." Pam had no fear of raising anger in her minions. In fact, she encouraged it.

"You dare insult my great-grandfather's legends?!" Petrakis declared. "I tell you, that Bulk is something supernatural. It is a dark monster of myth, the *vorvalaka!*"

"Well, whatever it is," Pam said, "prepare the facility for it. No one will stop us now."

"You are a fool!" spat Petrakis. "You are foolish for not fearing the *vorval*—"

Pam lifted him by the throat with one hand, as she had once with Alexis Legrande.

"This is what happens when you lose your temper around me," she told him. "Now. Prepare. The facility. For the Bulk."

And she threw him down with great force. Stunned to silence, he shuffled away, to rally his and Massillo's forces.

Pam was forced to admit to herself that Petrakis had a point. The Bulk *did* seem like something out of a myth, a fairy tale. But she knew he was the product of science, not magic or whatever power the mobster believed in.

Still, she had to wonder if there was such a thing as a *vorvalaka*. She was beginning to get suspicious of Vyrass.

But there were monsters of her own now available. Those Presidential supporters would once more prove useful.

CHAPTER 11

Hannah had insisted the pilot take them down in a field outside of Pam Demic's property, rather than at an actual airport. Hank was surprised how commanding his girlfriend could be, especially to her own employees. But he appreciated her confidence, even if he wished she'd been a bit more polite to the pilot.

"I shouldn't *have* to pay you double," she was saying, but she sighed and calmed down. Apologizing to the pilot, she sat comfortably as the aircraft took a sharp nosedive towards the edge of this strange stretch of Texan woods.

It was not a pleasant descent for the rest of the group. Ray and Hank both felt ill, and Sam and Blue's hands found each other as Sam's fear of heights tugged at him. But the pilot made it, thanks to the thoughts of money dancing in his mind.

"We're going to stage a full-frontal assault," Hannah explained. "But a stealthy one. We're staying away from guards and watching out for traps. And we're not carrying weapons."

"No weapons? What are we going to do if or when we find Pam Demic?" Ray asked.

"We have the *shadow* of a weapon," Hannah said. "Hank, that's where you come in."

"Ah—yes," Hank said. She'd explained this to him before

they'd boarded. He cleared his throat and said, "I am...going to fake that I am still the Bulk."

"That's a big bluff, guys," Sam said.

"But I think it's gutsy enough to work," Ray offered. "My brain is telling me that I know how to fight. I must remember that part of my training, deep down."

"And I can fight too," Blue said. "If this lady *is* behind this plague, it'll be more than a pleasure to knock her lights out."

"Fine," Sam said. "But like Hannah said, let's keep an eye out for traps."

Blue kissed Sam as they left the plane. It was a small thing but he kissed her back, warmly.

Ahead of them was the line of trees –they knew that Pam Demic's mansion was on the other side. They began making their way into those trees, slowly. Each of them silently wondered if their plane had been spotted, but they each chose to just keep their fingers crossed.

At first they didn't see any traps. They kept their eyes peeled for all sorts of danger—pressure pads, tripwires, laser eyes, everything they could think of. Their caution was beyond admirable. But it wouldn't guarantee perfection.

Ray couldn't be blamed for missing the device which met the underside of his shoe. Hank heard a faint metallic tick, and his head snapped down.

"Ray!" Hank cried. "Look out! Don't lift your foot!"

"Is it a mine?" Sam asked. Ray began to sweat.

Blue looked out into the woods. "*Incoming!*"

Out of the ground launched a number of catapults—the wooden arms slung perilous cargo towards the quintet. Ten eyes watched in horror as they saw the air was full of a flock of banana cream pies. One of these pies struck one of the trees, but it did not splut, as pies are wont to do—instead, with a thick crack, it split the trunk of the tall oak.

"Those pies have bricks in them!" Sam cried, his voice cracking. His arms raised to defend himself, in vain. But Blue moved quickly. She grabbed him by the shirt and ran, as Hank and Hannah and Ray ran.

Now there was no telling what was ahead of them. They had to focus on dodging the time-honored but greatly-feared symbols of classical cinematic humor.

And so it was that their feet pressed other hidden triggers, releasing other sinister devices. These ones were far more deadly. Bowling balls, anvils, and even steel safes became ammunition for the catapults hidden amongst the trees.

The group was used to running, each in their own way, but this was exhausting. The lethal projectiles were everywhere, smashing the large trunks around, and sending out sprays of wood chips. It was a nightmare.

But the terror was only just beginning.

They soon passed into the inner orbit of woods that surrounded the house of Pam Demic. Suddenly there were no more catapults, and the last of the weighted objects and pies smashed or splutted against the ground. But the five could now see a group of individuals ahead of them. These people shambled oddly, stiffly, as if awakening from a long slumber. It didn't take long to realize that these people were not normal.

"I can't believe it," Hannah whispered. "They look..."

Blue squinted. "Not good."

"They're murmuring something," Sam said. "Listen..."

"Nyuhhhhh..." said the oncoming creatures. "The South...shall rise...again..."

"Oh, no, they're brainless zombies!" Hank cried.

"Virus...came...from...China..." the zombies moaned.

"No, the virus here came from meatheads not wearing masks," said Hannah. "C'mon, guys. Let's bypass these creeps."

Rather than running away from the stumbling creatures, they ran towards them. They weren't afraid; once they were past them they'd have their chance at taking out the source of this plague.

But the zombies tried to stop them. Stumbling straight into their paths, the ghoulish creatures swiped their arms out at them.

"Get a job...hippie..." the zombies groaned, but their fingers failed to grab the encroaching heroes. "America...First..."

They had no cleverness in those clawing hands, no focus or wit in their undead eyes. The five were able to dodge their swings just by putting in a tiny bit of forethought. Maybe the terrain benefitted the zombies over the humans, but the living people were smart enough to punch through.

They kept running, seeing the end of the woods ahead of them. They refused to give up—the traps and the zombies proved to them that Pam Demic was behind the recent horror, and she would not go unpunished.

But there was one more horrific surprise awaiting them, once they finally cleared the trees. They thought that line of zombies was the last of them. But in truth they were just the first. The fields around the old mansion were rife with zombies, whole teeming hordes of them.

These zombies were just as hopeless as the others. It was just a matter of not getting overconfident—and not running headfirst into danger. The group, led by Hank, began weaving their way between the shuffling forms. They expected to see this sort of terror by night, but the Texan sun blazed overhead.

They kept an eye on the house. The enemy knew they were here—they could be planning something else for them. But there was no movement from the titanic mansion.

"Hank," Hannah whispered, "I'm glad you're with us. I wouldn't be able to do this alone."

"I love you," he said, and she grinned and echoed it back to him.

But then a zombie caught hold of Hannah's arm.

"Hank!" she cried, as the zombie tugged her towards itself.

Hank's eyes widened in horror. But his muscles reacted before his mind. Wrapping his arm tight in his sleeve, he snapped a punch out at one of the zombies. The blow lacked the strength of the Bulk, but it was sufficient to make the zombie lose its footing.

Its claws remained hooked on Hannah's shirt, but she escaped by tearing part of the fabric.

The foul things had closed in on the group in the time it took for her to get free. Sam and Hank tried to kick away the zombies, while Blue found it sufficient to pound them back with her fists.

They knew they couldn't win in a fight. More and more zombies lurched towards them. Overhead, they could now see a small squadron of zooming jet planes, which dropped zombies like bombs from above. The creatures plummeted towards the ground, with most landing intact. Unaffected by pain, they quickly rose up to begin their search for victims.

"We have to keep moving!" Hank cried, and once they each defeated their current target, they continued their run towards the house. They were almost there—they could see the rooms inside the mansion's windows.

It wasn't long before a new horror reared its head.

The zombies that patrolled the front door of the mansion were different. At least a few of them were. A figure strode out before the group, glaring at them with rotten eyes. It grinned with a familiar face—the face of Hannah's father.

Hank saw him at once. "General Darwin...?" he gasped. "Daddy?!" cried Hannah Darwin.

"Affirmative," sneered the General. He wore the military uniform he was buried in, and his trademark mustache hung gray under his nose.

"Hannah...I thought your father was dead," Sam murmured. "S-so did I..." Hannah replied quietly.

"Well, it seems I've been brought back as some sort of abomination of nature. That doesn't mean that I'm not at the top of this chain of command!" The General's bark was still as sharp as ever. "Hannah, at attention! Come join your father!"

"You're not my father," Hannah said simply. She ran up to him and pushed him over with all of her strength.

The General's arms were too stiff to lift him up. He wiggled on the ground helplessly, like a flipped tortoise.

"What is your major malfunction, daughter? I offer you a place of duty and honor serving on the front lines, and this is how you repay me?"

"This is too disturbing," Hank said, voicing what Hannah's shock kept her from saying. "We have to keep moving..."

But a voice shouted out:

"YOU—!"

To see General Darwin revived was bad enough for Hank. But now another ghost from his past stood before him. It wasn't possible—how had Pam Demic recovered both the General's corpse and *hers*...?

This ghoul was a woman. She had been dead longer than the General, and so her eyes were gone while his remained. But even without eyes, the woman's stare was full of hatred.

"You killed me!" the specter of Lisa Tuttle cried.

Ray Garton stared at the woman, and Hank saw his eyes light up. He knew that this woman was the ex-detective's former partner, who had died when the Bulk flipped a car on top of her. Beyond Hank's perception, Ray experienced a complete restoration of his memory. He looked at Hank, and knew that he was the Bulk. He looked at Lisa, and knew that Hank had killed her.

Lisa turned her head to look at the ex-amnesiac.

"Ray!" she howled. "You must avenge me. Kill Hank—kill the Bulk!"

Ray looked at Hank, who looked back at him. Their eyes stared icily into the depths of each others' for what seemed an eternity. Neither knew what the other would do.

Then, Ray ran. He dashed back into the hordes of zombies, away from Hank and the rest of them.

"Ray!" Hannah's voice reached Hank's ears, but he didn't hear it. He knew what had happened. And he felt shame.

But Lisa's ghoul wasn't done with them yet. She staggered towards them, as eager to eat them as her any of her other undead brethren.

"Keep—keep moving to the house," Sam directed breathlessly.

He saw that the group was winded, but he looked to Blue. "Help me," he pleaded her.

She reached out and picked him up with one arm. Looping him under that arm, she rallied her strength. She needed to get to Hank and Hannah. She'd carry one of them, just as the Bulk had carried Hannah and Sam before.

Blue knew, however, she was not as strong as the Bulk. She could only carry them a short distance before she collapsed. And now it seemed Hank was the one who'd have to find his own way. She was at Hannah's side, and she swept up the smaller woman with surprisingly ease.

Rallying all her focus, Blue marched forward almost mechanically. She ignored both the pain in her muscles and the zombies ahead of her. She sprinted to the front door, and kicked her way in. Then she toppled forward.

Hank was behind them. Blue's fall meant that Hannah and Sam were on the ground just outside the front entrance. The zombies lurking around the manor circled near them and began to close in. Hank cried out his girlfriend's name and ran up to the group. They quickly got onto their feet, and staggered into the house. Though Blue had broken the lock, they jerked the door closed behind them, and found that the zombies didn't know how to open the door once it was closed.

"I hope Ray's alright," Hank said.

"We have bigger things to worry about, my love," said Hannah. She pointed. A figure was walking confidently into large room in which they know stood.

Pam Demic was truly as gigantic as her pictures hinted. She was Blue's height, but she was different from Blue in many ways — the gold-flecked gleam in her eyes was much more sinister than the ocean-hued light in Blue's own orbs. She smiled at her guests.

"At last," she said. She pointed at Sam. "You! You must be Hank Howard."

"Ah, no, that's me, actually," said Hank, raising a hand."

"I'm Sam," Sam clarified.

"Oh, that's interesting. This one looks far stronger and more heroic than you," Pam said. "But then, I suppose, Dr. Jekyll was an unassuming fellow, until you got on his bad side. Which leads me to ask: why am I not seeing *your* bad side right now, Mr. Howard?"

"I don't know what you mean." Hank *did* know what she meant, but he wasn't going to say anything. He was looking for the other two people Hannah and Blue had mentioned, the white-clad woman and the green lady.

"I mean that you are the Bulk! Don't make me repeat myself, Hank Howard. You didn't transform as you attacked my complex.

I'm wondering why that is."

Hank didn't say anything, though sweat broke out on his forehead. Pam raised an eyebrow.

"You can't turn into him, can you? Either your earlier exploits against Dr. Kantlove were a display of special effects trickery...or you've lost your power..."

"I *will* become the Bulk," Hank said, "if you don't surrender to us, Pam Demic."

She laughed. "I'd love to battle your alter ego face-to-face.

I'm not afraid of him. I come from a line of strong women." Hank began to tremble, but nothing happened. Sam,

Hannah, and Blue looked at him expectantly, all while knowing they could expect nothing.

But then, Hank did surprise them. Without the Bulk, he ran straight at Pam, and slammed a punch as hard as he could muster into her chin.

She didn't move a muscle; there wasn't even a hint of her flinching. And Hank was left with a sore fist.

Once again Pam Demic laughed, before her arm shot out in a return punch. She sent Hank back flying.

Hannah cried out for her love, and once more dropped close to his side. He was bruised, but otherwise unhurt. All the same he knew he didn't stand a chance against such a finely trained woman.

But Hell hath no fury like a woman scorned, and Hannah Darwin was mighty scorned by the sight of her Hank laid out on the floor. She rose and charged towards her enemy, and Sam at once was with her. The two struck as one, and attacked the tall woman with blow after blow, punching and kicking and clawing. But they didn't even make a dent. It was like her tanned skin really was made of solid bronze. She threw Sam away, and then Hannah, as if they were nothing but rag-dolls.

Finally, there was Blue.

Their battle seemed fated, somehow. They had both trained for months and years and decades, building muscle through trial and pain and triumph. They had learned fighting styles which took the keenest of minds to master, and they had never faced an opponent they couldn't defeat before. For both of them, it would be a great insult to fall here.

They threw themselves at each other, grappling like titans of myth. Blue seized Pam by the arm and managed to throw her over her shoulder, aided by the latter's own strength. Pam had already started the fight on the wrong foot, and now she was tumbling through the air. Blue chased her down and as she tried to spring up, she grabbed her arm and lifted her up, only to toss her down again.

"Listen, my dear," Blue uttered, "the sooner you say uncle, the sooner it'll be o—"

Before she could say "—ver," Pam Demic seized her hands. She pulled her down to the ground, bringing Blue's face perilously close to her own. Then she brought the side of her hand into Blue's head, driving her aside. The ex-drill instructor rolled end over end, stunned. Pam rose, and closed in on her like a panther seeking her prey.

Blue, for once, felt a chill roll down her spine. She didn't know if she could beat Pam—she must have weighed near to two hundred pounds, and most of it was muscle. Plus she had the fighting skills of an Amazon. But Blue wasn't afraid of fighting dirty, not when so much depended on it. She kicked Pam hard in the gut, and sent her reeling for a moment. But only for a moment. Pam set upon again and pinned to the ground. Then, she threw down a knockout punch, and Blue saw stars.

"Your little game is over, it seems," Pam said. "My friend Vyrass will infect you with the plague, and you'll be off my back for good."

But there was a pressing question, which Pam couldn't answer yet: where was Vyrass?

CHAPTER 12

"Nein! Nein, don't you see! I *created* you! And now you must *obey* me!"

It was true that Vyrass was the creation of the man—or zombie—that stood before her. But she didn't see how that earned him a drop of her respect.

"I don't know why Pam decided to bring the zombies from Howard's hometown down here," Vyrass muttered to herself. "They've mostly proven to just be a nuisance."

The zombie of Dr. Werner von Kantlove stood before her, clad in both his familiar purple suit and his trademark monocle. His decaying body was looking pretty good for a man who'd suffered the fate he had. "How *dare* you call me a nuisance?!" he complained. "I am the greatest scientist the vorld has ever seen! The plague ravaging the vorld is by mein design!"

"Hey, you may have thought up the baby, but I delivered it," Vyrass said. "Alexis! I have something for you!"

"Ah, Alexis, ja-aa...I remember her very vell. I vonder if she is still as tasty-looking as I recall..." Kantlove had been trying to eat Vyrass for last ten minutes, but kept getting tripped up by his own monologues.

"Alexis!" Vyrass cried again. Her voice showed no fear, only irritation. "Listen, Can't-Love, I am my own woman now. These zombies are mine. This plague is mine. And now..." She laughed. "This world is mine."

Upon hearing the hated name "*Can't*-Love," Kantlove began to rage. "How *dare* you call me by zat name!" he ranted powerlessly. "I vill control you! I svear it to the gods of science!"

"No, *Can't*-Love," she said, grinning. She walked in circles around him, with great confidence in her steps. "I have my own designs. And neither that foolishly-named woman downstairs nor the little fool in white who's on her way now have any idea what's coming."

"You vould betray your own comrades?" hissed Kantlove. Then he grinned. "Ja, that is *very* evil! Vell done!"

Vyrass put a finger to her lips to shush him. At that moment, Alexis Legrande broke down the door to Vyrass' room.

"Destroy this zombie," she ordered, and Alexis immediately drew one of her cunning blades. She threw it with an assassin's precision, lodging it between Kantlove's shoulder blades. His sliced muscles collapsed and the zombie lost use of his legs.

Kantlove screamed out, "Mein Fuhrer! I can't walk!" Alexis stepped over to him and picked up the pair of garden shears that Vyrass kept as a trophy from her first murder. Even the plague-woman had to look away when Alexis parted Kantlove's head from his body.

But the zombie of Vyrass' mad creator was far from dispatched, as Kantlove's severed head continued talking. "Now, listen here, little missy, you are in big trouble!" he barked at her. "Sew me back on to mein body, *und macht schnell!*"

"No thanks," Vyrass said. "I'll leave the Frankenstein stuff to you, doctor. I mean, I imagine it'll be tough to do without..."

"You are a little minx, you know this?" Kantlove cursed. He closed his eyes, and before Alexis and Vyrass could say anything his headless body lifted itself up off the ground.

"Mein father used to say, you're nobody if you've got no

body," Kantlove laughed. "Now—let's go see vhat is happening downstairs."

The body moved towards the open door and began to bumble its way towards the staircase. Vyrass looked at Alexis and growled in irritation. Kantlove was lost in a fit of insane laughter, but Alexis stuffed him behind a pillow on Vyrass' bed. She wasn't looking forward to Pam's reaction to all this.

Vyrass heard Pam talking to some people down below. As she crossed down the stairs she got a quick peek around the corner, before she hid herself. There were two men and two women, all of whom had been thoroughly socked into submission by Pam's mighty fists. Vyrass sensed they weren't infected, which was repulsive to her. She'd make sure to give these interlopers a double dose of her plague.

But first, she wanted to see how Pam would react to an unscheduled interruption.

Dr. Kantlove's body sprinted down the stairs into the main chamber. Pam turned and her eyes widened. She recognized that unmistakable suit from pictures. Though he was missing his head, she knew exactly who this cadaver belonged to.

In her brief moment of shock, the body encircled its hands around her throat. She immediately began fighting back against the ghoul, turning away from her charges in the process.

Slowly, Hank, Hannah, Sam, and Blue got to their feet, and began to creep away. Pam leveled punch after punch at Kantlove's undead form, but somehow couldn't get loose from his grip. Her four prisoners exited the house quickly, choosing the perils of the zombie-field over another match with the bronze giantess.

Vyrass enjoyed a private laugh at seeing Pam proven fallible.

As soon as the four were gone, Pam destroyed the body of the Kantlove zombie.

"Where's the head?" she cried. "Alexis! Vyrass! *Where is the head?!*"

Vyrass emerged from her hiding spot—Alexis had been

camping out on the stairs. They pointed Pam up to Vyrass' bedroom, where Alexis had stashed the mad scientist's head.

Pam found her quarry by honing in on his maniacal rants. "—und so, having thus flooded the Grand Canyon, I vill commence the bombardment of every Applebee's in the vorld mit gamma rays..." Pam pulled back the pillows concealing the head. "Ahh! Nein! Vhat are you doing?!"

Pam stomped over the nearest window, and smashed it with her fist. "This is the end of you, *Can't*-Love!"

"That's *KANT*...oh, never mind." groaned the zombified head. "I'm dead, aren't I?"

"Yes, you impotent fool!" Pam cried.

Then, with all her strength, she hurled the head of Dr. Kantlove out into the woods, where she was sure it struck a mine.

Vyrass waited a beat before she said, "I hate to say this but the heroes escaped."

"I *know*," said Pam Demic then. "I saw them escape. Find them! Track them down! I want Hank Howard and his compatriots dead by tomorrow's sunrise!"

Vyrass grinned, suppressing a deep laugh. Then, with a strange look in her yellow eyes, she said, "Of course, mistress. Anything you say."

CHAPTER 13

The quartet were forced back to their plane, which took off immediately. They would need to stop over in a nearby city to refuel, but then they planned to head back to Chez Darwin. There was nothing else they could do.

"We still don't even have proof that she was behind the virus," Blue sighed.

"Yeah. She only barely confessed. If we told anyone important about it, they wouldn't believe us without a recording," added Hannah.

"And we lost Ray," said Hank.

It seemed hopeless. Now there were zombies, as well as a deadly plague.

"We can't give up, guys," Sam implored. "We have to believe that there's still a way."

"I mean, we could always just quarantine, wear masks, and wait for a vaccine, I suppose," Blue said.

"That's reasonable," Hank said. "Actually, that really is what we should be doing. But we still owe it to ourselves to defeat Pam Demic."

"I think Hank is right. She's dangerous, evidently, and she

won't stop until someone stops her," said Hannah. "Even if it's the harder thing to do, we have to try again."

"We need more people," Blue said. "Strong ones. No offense to you guys—especially since I got knocked down too—but I did carry most of that fight."

Sam opened his mouth to say something about a certain purple former comrade of theirs, but remained silent. Still, Hank knew what he was thinking—and he was sure that Hannah and Blue were thinking the same thing. It was hard for him not to laugh.

Once, Hannah had feared the Bulk, to the point where she'd implied an end to their engagement over him. Now, it seemed she wanted him back more than ever.

He was beginning to see what Sam had told him about.

There had been good in his gigantic alter ego—because at his core, he was still him. He still guided the Bulk, even as he rampaged; he had been the one stopping him from crushing people under his feet or smashing innocents with his pounding fists. He could only see how much control he had now that he was separated from his other self.

He was about to open his mouth, but just then, the lights went out.

"Damn!" Sam cried. "What now?"

"Maybe I should go check the breakers..." Hannah said. But they all knew somehow that it wasn't that. When the TV came on by itself, they almost expected it.

"Hello, my fellow Americans," said Pam Demic over the screen. "If you live in one of the major cities we've selected for our little test, you may have noticed that you are experiencing a power failure. I have decided to incapacitate those in charge of supplying electricity to your cities, as part of my extended demands. I suppose I should clarify what demands I mean, and how I have the authority to make them.

"I am responsible for the pandemic which you have been experiencing. I can stop its spread just as easily as I started it, but I will need money to do so. I expect your cities to turn over their entire treasuries to me and my associates at the earliest convenience. Ask for me in Texas. You'll find me, don't worry—or maybe it's that I'll find you?

"My comrades and I eagerly await payment. I don't really think there's anything I need to elaborate on. Do not attempt to kill us. Many armies around the world have plotted my assassination, and all have failed. So anyway. Thank you all for listening so politely. Toodle-oo!"

Then the broadcast cut out, leaving the TV as dead as every other appliance in the house.

For a long time, the group sat in silent darkness. They tried not to give in to their hopelessness, but they couldn't find anything to say that wasn't horrifically pessimistic.

Blue went to go find a flashlight, but found that it was as dead as the wires lining the walls. She changed the batteries, but it was no good. She called back to the others: "She's shorted out wireless devices, too!"

Sure enough, all of their cell phones had lost their charge.

At last, Hannah exclaimed, "Oh, sweet God, I'm gonna panic. I don't know what to do."

"We can't do nothing," Sam said. "We can't just give up here. Not after everything we've done. We've got to work on a plan to—"

Sam's words quickly faded away from Hank's ears as he once more contemplated the feelings within him. Having been interrupted before, he had to work up his courage again...

But there was another interruption. The opening of the front door.

They all froze when they heard the sound. It could be someone seeking to take advantage of the power outage. Perhaps someone in Pam Demic's employ.

As they each slowly rose from the table, they saw the arcing beam of a flashlight sweep into the room. Its bearer made a small noise, and found his way to them. They all cried out in surprise upon seeing his face.

"Ray!"

Ray Garton waved an anxious hello. "I didn't want to shout in case you were still expecting Pam's agents."

"I mean, sneaking in like a burglar doesn't help with that fear," Hannah said. But then she smiled. "I'm glad you came back, Ray."

Before Hank could say anything—and he had a lot to say—Sam started talking.

"How did you get your flashlight to work? She shorted out all the batteries here. My guess is some sort of nanotechnology is involved…"

Ray's face was serious. "The police get a lot of military gadgets these days. That includes these special 'Gale' batteries. They're wind-powered; you blow into them to recharge them."

He was talking the same way he did when he excitedly showed off a new app he'd found on his phone. But he had none of his previous humor.

His head snapped up. "Hank. We need to talk."

"Let's talk," Hank agreed. He stood, and approached his friend. At once, Hank said, "I am so, so sorry for what I did to your partner."

"I know you are, Hank. That's why I came back."

"Do you have all your memories now?"

He nodded. "I remember everything about my past life. I remember how much I hated you for what you did to Lisa. But my amnesia gave me the chance to see you with fresh eyes, for who you really are."

He set his hands on Hank's shoulders. "You're a good man, Hank Howard. I should have tried to *help* you before, because you were struggling with the Bulk. He brought you pain, and all I had for you was meanness. But I want all that to change. I know you're sorry, Hank. I'm sorry too."

And he pulled him in for a hug.

Hank was glad to have his friend back. It would make saying this next part easier.

"I have a suggestion to make," he said, forcing the words out. "And as I've apologized to Ray, I would like to apologize to each of you before I make it." He looked at Sam. "I'm sorry, old buddy, that I made you do so much lab work, only to have to undo it."

"Undo it?" Sam asked, but Hank went on:

"Blue, I'm sorry that I was so harsh when you told us about Pam Demic. I should have trusted you better."

"No worries, Hank! I'm in Ray's camp, I've always known you were a good person," Blue said.

At last Hank set eyes on the most important person. "I'm sorry, Hannah, for—"

"Shush." And she kissed him. That was all that was needed.

"So..." Sam said at once, "I take it you're interested in...becoming the Bulk again?"

"Yes," Hank said quietly.

Sam nodded. "I'm glad you finally kicked the rocks out of your head and saw the light. Let's do it."

Hank grinned, as Hannah and Blue agreed with Sam. "But there's an issue," Sam said, joining Ray and Hank in standing. "We need our original documentation on Serum-114 to recreate the experiment that turned you into the Bulk in the first place."

"Oh. That's true," said Hank, looking downward.

"It's a good thing, though, that last night I finally picked up the necessary papers."

Sam produced a folder of documents which he had recovered from the ruins of their lab.

"What?" Hank exclaimed. "How did you get those? And when?"

"Last night," Sam said, finally allowing himself a trickster's smile. "A little while back I found a safe buried in the rubble that had once belonged to General Darwin—but I would have to blow up the lock to open it. So I decided to be patient. And while we were in Texas, the Army retracted their guard around the lab ruins. So I went in there and blew the safe."

"You went in there last night?" Hank asked. "You *anticipated* this, you jerk!"

"I did," laughed Sam. "Now, do you want me to tell you about the weirdness or do you want to read about it yourself ?"

"Spoil us," said Hank.

"The element we were missing is an example of exotic matter. It's a crystalline substance which was discovered and experimented on by scientists in New Mexico. The General was able to get us a sample only through a lot of finagling. He kept us in the dark about what we were working with."

"That must be the element our 'cure' serum neutralized," Hank said.

"Exactly," Sam replied. "We were really lucky to chance on a solution to that element, because no one really knows anything about it. In fact, the notes suggest that it may not even come from Earth."

"What?!" Hank exclaimed, joined by the others.

"Yeah, it gets a little esoteric...something about a bridge to the Chaos Rift?"

"What the hell is the Chaos Rift?" asked Hank, entirely shocked. "That doesn't sound like science to me."

"Ah, well, apparently the depths of the Multiverse contains a, uh, a 'blazing conflagration of untamed energies such as those seen at the dawn of new universes, spanning the width of many realities and exerting the corresponding gravity of such.'" He shrugged. "Makes sense to me."

"So, this Rift, whatever it is—somehow I received its energies, through the serum?"

"I think so."

"And here I was thinking we were just building on steroid compounds from the '40s," sighed Hank. "I didn't know that General Darwin had something a bit more modern on his hands."

"Knowing my father, I have a feeling he got that space- crystal thing under nefarious circumstances," Hannah said bitterly.

"Speaking of the space-crystal," Sam said, "guess what else was being kept in the lab safe this whole time?"

At once, he produced a large object and tossed it onto the table. It appeared to be an enormous orange geode, which sparkled like a candle under Ray's flashlight-beam.

"Amazing!" Blue cried, kissing Sam on the cheek.

"I'll echo that—admittedly without the kiss," Hannah said. "We can create the serum now, and strike back at Pam! Right?"

Sam shook his head. "It's not that simple. The files reminded me that some of the chemicals we put into the serum could only be rendered through lab equipment which we don't have time to procure. Plus, we can't power them. So I don't think we can recreate the chemical."

"What can we do then?" Hank asked.

"Well, apparently, under the right light frequencies—the, uh, molecular nature of the crystal is agitated. It creates dimensional warps."

Ray pulled his flashlight away from the crystal. Sam laughed. "I don't think it's *that* unstable. We'd need to build something to emit the right frequency. But that's one machine we'd be building, next to the two or three we'd need for the chemical mixture."

"I think I know what sort of machine you're talking about, pal," Hank said. "I'm pretty sure we could build it from appliances around the house, plus a few bits from the cars. But powering it is another thing." He looked at Ray. "How many of those Gale batteries do you have?"

"Uh, I have a twelve-pack from Megalomart. I can go out and buy more if I have to."

"We're gonna need as much power as we can get," said Hank. "So maybe go get another twelve-pack."

Ray nodded, and turned to leave. As he did so, however, Hank cleared his throat.

"Let's all have a drink first. Because I'm glad you came back."

Ray grinned and Hannah went down to her dad's wine cellar. The work that followed went a lot smoother than the long period of trial and error that went into the formation of a cure.

Hank and Sam were more inspired than ever, aided now by their romantic muses. Hannah and Blue were just as much a part of the process as the two scientists. They helped gather pieces from around the Darwin mansion, and supplied physical labor in putting the machine together. They worked by candlelight, wanting to save as many of those batteries as they could. Ray kept guard against any agents of evil who sought to disturb their work.

It took only four days for them to build the machine they needed. They had no way of testing if the light it emitted was at the right frequency. They just had to hope for the best.

They had chosen one of the parlors for their test, to prevent external light contamination. Once they were ready, Sam needed to prime the machine in absolute darkness, while Hank stood before the emitter, whose lens was made of the Chaos Rift crystal.

Over the last few days, they had discussed how they had no idea what would happen. But by now Hank was used to being the subject of risky experiments. However, this *was* the first time he was creating a dimensional warp; for all he knew this warp would spawn a black hole and the whole Earth would be destroyed. Or he'd end trapped in some other cosmos, unable to return.

But it would be worth it. Pam Demic needed to be stopped. They couldn't afford to hesitate any longer.

Their machine looked like a long-barreled gun of some kind, mounted conspicuously on a large steel box. They each inspected their creation skeptically, as one by one, Ray snuffed out the candles. Sam held Blue close to him, and Hank enjoyed what he feared was a final embrace with Hannah. But they were ready. Sam knew how to run the control console, and in silence, he set everything into position.

Hank watched the far wall from his position between it and

the machine. Invisible particles streamed through and around him, and when they connected with the wall, they released minute quantities of light. These lights began to swarm like insects around the blank surface.

"Wow..." Hannah whispered. "It's beautiful..."

The lights glowed with every color of the rainbow, and spread out more and more as the treated light traveled through the unusual lens. In the air was the faint smell of gasoline, or diesel-fuel, despite the fact that their engine worked on batteries.

Suddenly, the wall seemed to cave into itself, forming a tunnel of light—a glowing psychedelic portal. Hank knew this was his transport. He started walking towards the strange doorway.

The odyssey began.

At first, it seemed to Hank like the closer he walked towards the portal, the farther away it got from him. That was when he saw that the edges of the room around the portal were bending into the portal, elongating as they did so. The room was swiftly transforming into a long tunnel, with the portal at the end. Hank wondered if he could ever reach the glowing doorway—it forever receded, like the castle of Ysbaddaden Bencawr of Welsh mythology, or even, perhaps more legendarily, the infinite staircase of *Super Mario 64.*

Then the portal reared up and swallowed him, before he was ready. He was cast into a dark void.

But the void did not remain dark for long. Suddenly, on either side of him, there appeared long, streaming stretches of light—neon tubes packed into rectangular strips, like endless circuit boards. They rushed past him at unimaginable speed, and as he gazed headlong into their path, he felt like he was falling down a bottomless shaft.

Around him sang an eerie choir of countless voices, singing out something classical. It seemed less like music than like an incarnate portent of doom.

He stared, mouth agape, blinded by the glory.

It was like every circuit of his brain was on fire. Every sensation he'd ever felt, every memory he'd ever lived, was alive in his mind. He tasted lemonade and soda from his childhood summers, chilling with his cousins Hugh and Garth over at Aunt Lota's house; he smelled the rubber on the pencil eraser he chewed during his high school physics test, and in his eyes flashed the clear images of every flower he'd ever looked at. He remembered his first kiss with Hannah—he remembered every kiss with her. But it was all too much. He felt like his entire nervous system was melting.

The luminescent circuitry passed him by for what seemed like an eternity, before it just suddenly snapped off. But his reeling mind was plunged into a yet deeper layer of the cosmos around him. Once more there was a chilling darkness, like empty space— but light came into it again, a light emitted from the unbelievable sights before him.

All around him was a series of pulsating globules of star- dust, nebulae and galaxies formed of a shapeless, half-real jelly. The blank darkness suddenly now appeared to be a pale mauve, which faintly churned like boiling hops. This was the very heart of the Chaos Rift. The birthplace of gods and monsters, the cradle of madness given form.

The longer he stared into this abyss, the longer it seemed to stare back. His brain, struggling for reference in this uncanny place, began to create shapes out of the bacteria-shaped lights and lava- lamp paisleys. This cloud-gazing in the crystal-freckled voids before him created the shapes of a World War I flying ace; Robin Hood shooting an arrow; a gecko typing at a laptop; Zeus and his thunderbolts; a flying dog in a cape; and many others. Hank struggled to close his eyes, but every inch of him was paralyzed.

Then there were voices in the silence. The words of mystic sages whispered out to him, like in the occult tales of yore. He tried to block them out, but they came anyway.

"One morning I shot an elephant in my pajamas. How he got in my pajamas, I dunno..."

"There's a thousand reasons why I shouldn't drink, but I can't think of one right now..."

"Once, during Prohibition, I was forced to live for days on nothing but food and water..."

"I was dreaming I was awake, and then I woke up and found myself asleep..."

"HEY, ABBOTT...!"

At last the paralysis broke, and Hank pressed his hands over his eyes and ears.

The noise stopped, but it took him a long while to look around again.

The void was gone. Instead, he was standing in a white room —its brightness stunned his eyes for a moment, and when they cleared he saw how formal this room looked. At each of the walls were soft-looking chairs, and against one of the broad walls was a large bed, about queen-size, albeit a little smaller. There was a small dining table near the bed, overlaid with a patterned table-cloth. The ceiling stood on top of a series of Grecian columns, and paintings from the Renaissance and Romantic periods hung between these pillars. Busts and statuettes of unknown Greco-Roman figures also adorned the room. The chamber was large enough where it felt somehow empty, even with all of these deco-rations.

For what seemed an eternity, Hank stared around the room.

Then he looked down at his hands, wondering if an eternity had indeed passed. His hands looked wrinkled with age, and as he brought them to his face, he felt the coarse skin of an older man. Somehow, this didn't perturb him in any way. He saw a doorway (had it been there before?) leading out into a corridor of some kind. He began to walk towards it.

Passing through the corridor, he found himself back in the original chamber. But this time, something was different. Only barely acknowledging the looped nature of the corridor in his mind, Hank observed an old man eating at the dining table. From what he could see, it looked to be some kind of pot roast, with potatoes and carrots. He approached the old man, who began to speak.

"You too, eh?" the old man said.

Hank frowned in confusion, but found he could not speak. "All of our kind come here at some point. It is perhaps a part of us."

The old man sipped a glass of wine.

"Surely you did not imagine you were the first of the transforming champions? We have always existed, throughout history. In the olden days, we were called berserkers, or, as time went on, trolls. We were known for our rages, wherein we warped into monsters. Or gods."

In all this time the old man hadn't look at Hank, and he continued to stare forward.

"My god abandoned me here, after he found his Valhalla. Or perhaps not—he did not die in battle, but in a cancer ward. Leaving me here, as I was always meant to be." Another sip of wine. "But I believe he went to the warriors' heaven."

Between the man's words there was true silence—there wasn't the familiar buzz of electricity, or the sound of water pipes. It dawned on Hank that there wasn't a toilet in this place.

"We pass in many ways," the old man started to say.

He set his wine glass down, but his arthritis-swollen fingers slipped. The glass fell to the ground and shattered. The old man hunched down to the fractured glass, and stared at it, as if something horrific had just come to pass.

Just then Hank stood in his place, looking up now at the room's bed. There was a figure in it, who Hank recognized as a yet older incarnation of the old man. Only now did he realize that the old man resembled himself.

"We do not appear at random," said the man, whose voice was slowed by its owner's impending death. "But we are not chosen either."

Hank still couldn't speak. Probably a good thing, as his companion didn't have much time left.

"We emerge from the shadows when we are required," said the old man. "When a voice in need calls."

Now he was beginning to glow. Hank blinked, raising his hand to his eyes as the light grew brighter and brighter. Somehow, the words etched themselves like stone carvings into Hank's mind, and they were all he could focus on.

When we are needed...

"You are still needed. You cannot shirk a gift that still has necessity..."

"She needs me," Hank said, as if realizing the fact for the first time. "Hannah needs me."

"The world," uttered the old man, and that was all. He raised a feeble, emaciated hand, as if he saw something invisible and terrible before him. Then he was gone, consumed by the golden light.

No—he wasn't gone. In his place, and in place of the room, was a wide-eyed infant, cocooned in a glowing bubble. Hank stared upon it, witnessing that his hands were returned to normal. Then he looked down. They seemed to be in orbit over the Earth. He never thought he'd see the stars again.

He gazed at this child born of stars, and the child gazed back. Then, once more, the child fell into golden light—but this light inverted, becoming purple instead. With eyes full of wonder, Hank reached out towards the light, calling it into himself. And he smiled; that smile broke into a laugh. The first time he felt this tickle, it was corrupted, as he'd been so scared of dying from his own serum. But now he realized that his power was far more pure than he'd previously realized. He'd trekked through Chaos and learned the truth, however slippery and vague it seemed. At his heart, protecting Hannah was his first priority. It was the soul of him.

And he would keep her safe as the Bulk.

The light grew and grew, and then collapsed on itself. Hank was back in the laboratory. Hannah, Sam, Blue, and Ray stared at him, struck silent by his new appearance.

Before they could say anything, Hank grinned and closed his eyes. At his command, he summoned the tornado of transformation, which replaced him with the Amazing Bulk. But this time things were different. Now Hank felt himself not as a murky half-presence within the Bulk, but as a sober and conscious mind, steering the gigantic purple form all by himself. His friends continued to stare at him, having let out a cry of surprise when he changed. He knelt down in front of Hannah, whose breathing accelerated, quite against her will. She stared into his eyes.

"Hank?"

He smiled, and extended a giant hand towards her. She realized what he meant, and put her own hand out. Hers was only big enough to shake one of his fingers—but it was a handshake all the same.

"Evil had better watch out," Sam said proudly. "'Cause he's back! The Amazing Bulk returns!"

The Bulk beat his chest like a bull ape, and let out a triumphant roar. Then, with the same ease as before, he changed back to Hank.

It was time to really focus now. They had some planning to do.

CHAPTER 14

Once the plan was agreed, on the quintet got to work. Hannah's pilot took a solitary passenger back to Texas, where Pam Demic and friends had set up camp. Hank, now alone, was going to perform a stunt he'd tried out once before, during the siege of Castle Kantlove. If he'd survived one jump out of a plane sans parachute, what would stop him from making two?

The pilot, Trent, wasn't pleased with the idea, but he didn't know that Hank was the Bulk. In fact, he'd never even heard of the Bulk in his life. He was understandably quite shocked when he turned the plane around, and saw a large purple mass of muscle in the place of Hank Howard. But lacking reference, he had no idea what to tell people.

Things would be very different this time. The Bulk wasn't afraid of any of Pam's traps. He wasn't afraid of her green woman, Vyrass, nor her white-clad assassin, Alexis. He broke into a run, taking off at top speed. His running pose, which kept his arms tucked at his sides, looked stiff and awkward, and yet his legs carried with tremendous velocity. As he passed into the woods surrounding the mansion, he began to set off the traps.

One by one, mines blew around him; swinging trees sharpened to spikes bounced off his impervious skin; deep pits served only as minor annoyances. He was moving fast, too, much faster than his colossal size seemed to allow. He left a river-ribbon of fallen trees trailing behind him.

Then came the men with guns. The Bulk tried to steer clear of them, or else smash the ground near them—the impact sent them reeling, but uninjured. Their bullets, of course, were nothing more than raindrops against his skin. Hank was still getting used to his newfound sense of control—it was beyond delightful to feel completely invulnerable, to feel the strength of ten giants coursing through him.

They had tanks this time, blasting him from afar—the shells were as ineffective as the bullets, turning into oversized coins once they hit him. One of the tank drivers got it in their mind that getting closer would make the shells more effective. The Bulk released a loud noise that almost sounded like a laugh. The tank's gun barrel was little more than a handle for him to grab onto—he lifted the crawling machine over his head, and hurled it into the horde of tanks ahead of him. He didn't even really have to do it, but it was a demonstration.

Next came the aircraft: planes, helicopters, even a few birds that looked like proto-spaceships, including flying saucers. When had Pam Demic had the time to dream up all this stuff? More likely it was stolen Kantlove technology.

But all they had was bullets and bombs, and neither of those were effective against the Bulk's impenetrable hide. Even the strange high-tech guns on the spaceships, which fired lightning bolts and crimson lasers, did nothing to him. He wanted to take to the air all the same.

When one of the planes swooped low to try to bomb him, he grabbed onto its undercarriage, letting it take him into the sky. He was heavy, so the plane was starting to sink—but a squadron which had formed up below him, and he only needed to get as far as their formation. He dropped down, and used planes and flying saucers as stepping stones as he skipped innocently through the air. The impact of his heavy feet shattered the midsection of each of the planes, sending them plummeting towards the ground. The pilots had sense to bail out, but now Pam Demic's lawn was scattered with the burning remnants of scores of aircraft.

Using his amazing leaps, the Bulk rampaged across the airfleet until only a few ships remained in flight. The Bulk did not know that down below, one of Pam Demic's lieutenants was escaping with a gigantic suitcase full of embezzled money. Johnny Clay wiped his sweating brow, as he watched the battle overhead. He wasn't about to let some giant purple monster rub him out. Pam's empire was finished. It was time to get out of there.

In his case he had most of the ransom money that had been paid to Pam and the two other women. Those cities, naturally, had acted quickly to get their electricity back. And now it was all going straight into Johnny Clay's bank account.

He came from a long line of criminals, like many of Pam's servants, and he was sure he'd done his forebears proud. He was dreaming of all the stuff he'd spend the money on. All he'd ever wanted was now at his fingertips. It was just a matter of avoiding any slip-ups—

Just then, a small dog rushed out ahead of him. Distantly, Johnny recognized it as Stanley, Dr. Kantlove's pet pug. He had no idea how he'd gotten here, but the little mutt placed himself right in the way of his next step. He tripped, and as he toppled forward, the briefcase broke open. Hundreds of hundred-dollar bills rushed out of the case like fall leaves out of a torn bag. Johnny was flooded with terror, and this feeling only deepened when he saw one of the large planes diving down towards the money.

He was sure that the turbines would blow it all away. All his fabulous money! He couldn't let it happen—but what could he do?

Instead of being blown away, however, the money instead flew up, sucked into the whirling force of the turbines. Once it was all swallowed, smoke erupted from the great engines, and suddenly they exploded. The plane angled down towards the mansion, and Johnny covered his eyes and ears.

The plane smashed into the house's roof.

In an instant, the entire building fell level, and a plume of flames reached out towards the sky like a scarlet hand. Rubble and dust spiraled upward, like one of the Bulk's tornadoes. This flying debris took care of the last of Pam Demic's fleet.

Johnny Clay was suddenly thankful to be alive. He ran far from the burning house, hoping to make a killing a safer way.

The Bulk hit the ground, unharmed. He roared up at the now-blackened sky, before sprinting towards the ruins of the house. Maybe this meant the mastermind behind the plague was destroyed.

But he had a strange feeling he had no such luck. Some important people had been left behind, however.

His enemy's three generals were sprawled on the ground, next to the wreckage of the jeep they'd tried to escape in. They'd been caught in the very edge of the blast. Gaetano and Massillo were dead. Petrakis barely clung to life.

He saw the Bulk loom over him, but his face was stern and serious. "I do not fear you any longer, *vorvalaka*," he said. "For I fear Pam Demic's green monster much more. Your power fails you..." He groaned. "My mistress has already fled this place, with her two comrades. She...left us to die, it seems. By now she will have kidnapped your four companions..."

The Bulk wanted to question him, but was unable to speak—and he knew there wasn't time to change back to Hank. He could only stare with his massive eyes as Petrakis began to laugh, however thinly.

"I know...that she knows...how you care...about the girl..." And with that, Petrakis expired.

The Bulk grimaced, knowing that if he didn't move fast, Hannah and the others were doomed.

Fortunately, the Bulk was anything but slow.

* * *

Media coverage across the country was unable to explain the strange purple shape reported by dozens of individuals across the country. Farmers and the people of a few small towns reported seeing a blur of purple arc rushing past them at 200 miles per hour. Some whose eyes were sharper than most spotted a shape within that blur—a strange, humanoid figure, who clutched his arms close to him and staggered somewhat as he ran. "He looked ridiculous," one witness specified, "holdin' his arms in like he was constipated or somethin'."

The Bulk was pushing his incredible abilities to their limits. He didn't have a second to spare, and taking a plane back as Hank Howard would be too slow. So instead he made his own way in the world.

He didn't want to think of what Pam Demic had planned for his friends. For his fiancée. For his city. She was a fast mover— no doubt she'd already filled the streets with traps, like the ones he'd seen before. But he knew these would like mosquitoes trying to drink the blood out of a boulder. Even as he crossed hundreds of miles, he wasn't even close to being tired.

Soon he was at the edge of his hometown, sprinting down one of its roads. He passed the woods where they met Blue, and the turn in the freeway that led to where her grandfather lived— where he'd reunited with Garton. His enormous heart pounded harder the closer he got to his friends.

At the city's edge, two gigantic anti-aircraft guns waited for him. The bullets they fired were huge, but they were like foam darts to the Bulk. In a blur of motion and force, he tore the twin guns from their mounts and threw them into the air like he was a carnival juggler. They slammed against each other heavily, and fell to the ground in pieces. The Bulk had no time to admire the wreckage; he dashed away from it and crossed on the city's first street.

Mines sprang up in the road in front of him, but they weren't primed to explode. While flying through the air they split open like clams and machine guns popped out. The Bulk just ran past them and the blaze of gunfire they let out, but his leg tangled in a tripwire along the way. A catapult launched a large metal sphere towards him. It attracted to his body as if by magnetism.

When it touched him, hundreds of thousands of volts erupted from inside the metal casing. The Bulk cried out but only in surprise. The strong electricity only tickled. All the same, he crushed the device in his huge hands.

At this rate it would take him forever to explore the city. It was time to take a higher perspective.

The Bulk ran deeper into the metropolis, and as he did so he became bigger and bigger. More of the fighting machines he'd faced in Texas appeared before him, but by the time he was done growing, they were smaller than toys. Indeed, if they had been toys, they would be considered choking hazards with how small they were to him. They unleashed an inferno of gunfire, and the Bulk did all he could to protect the buildings. But it was inevitable that some of the city was damaged.

At last he reached a mound of rubble in the center of the city, with three figures standing atop it. They had to be Pam Demic, Alexis Legrande, and Vyrass. They were gesturing at a missile-bearing helicopter to take off—it was one of the last flying craft they had left. For all their efforts to transform the city, they had failed to build traps that could stop him.

That was when the helicopter fired its rockets. He observed briefly that their warheads were tipped with a familiarly-colored material. He realized too late that the orange-hued lumps were made of Chaos Rift crystals.

When the missiles struck them he swore he felt the full force of their blasts. For the first time, the Bulk felt pain—as if he were naught but a mortal man. His dazed shock caused him to lose size, shrinking to nearly half his original height.

The pilot kept a bead drawn on his massive target, and fired a second missile. The Bulk tried to block it with his hands, but that only meant his hands felt the pain. Once more he shrank down, until he was only about ten feet tall.

The chopper dropped low and began to stalk him, waiting for another chance to open fire on him. He still had his speed, though, and he put it to good use. That pilot would have to work hard to bring him down.

How had Pam Demic learned of his connection to the strange quartz of the Chaos Rift? Maybe she had some secret helper, a fourth member of her band, advising her from afar. The Bulk couldn't stop to think about it. He just had to take down that copter before it could shoot another missile.

Too late—he heard the sound of ignition behind him, and wheeled fast around the corner. He only barely escaped the missile's blast, and fortunately, the street was empty.

If there was a building large enough to house him, he could hide until the right time. He suddenly had an idea, and found an alley to duck into. While the helicopter wheeled around to track him, he quickly changed back to Hank Howard—he managed to make his transformation tornado come and go in a hurry, speeding its movement up like a Keystone Kops short. Then he found some trash cans to hide behind.

To the chopper, it seemed like the Bulk disappeared into thin air, and in a sense he had. Hank waited till the chopper passed over him—then, muting his tornado again, he turned back. His powerful legs pushed him high into the air, and he grabbed the tail of the chopper. It cracked under his great weight, and without balance in the tail, the copter's flying days were done. The Bulk only had to leap clear and let gravity do the rest.

As a deafening explosion consumed the crashed chopper, the Bulk turned around to head back to where he'd seen Pam Demic and her cohorts. He took off running again, but as he passed back through the alley which had hid him from his aerial attacker, a darting shape lunged out of the darkness towards him.

Alexis Legrande had waited all this time to show off how fast she was. And how deadly. In her hand was a dagger, but it wasn't any ordinary knife. It was made of the same orange crystal as the heads of those rockets. To the Bulk's shock, the blade pierced his skin with ease, and the pain that flooded him was unbelievable.

"Gonna krovv you like a fat-*brookoed* pig, my son," Alexis laughed. "Made a nozh of glimmer-crystal, I have. And I'm too skorry for your punching."

The Bulk tried to hit her, but as she'd warned, she easily ducked out of the way. As she did so she raked her blade across the Bulk's arm, cutting him again.

The pain was incredible, but the Bulk couldn't give up. He tried to grab Alexis, and dodged her attempted strike when he failed. He threw a few more futile punches in the strange woman's direction, but couldn't connect.

The only issue was that Alexis tired, and the Bulk didn't.

And the Bulk could take a lot of hits from that little dagger—while Alexis would be down in one. She cut the Bulk again and again, but this only made him madder. And there seemed to be a direct correlation between his rage and his level of strength.

Then he got the lucky hit. Alexis tried to get a cut in on his torso, but the Bulk swatted her away—and she went flying the distance of a city block. "You bolnoy bolshy bratchy *boojum*!" she shrieked as she sailed into the sky.

The Bulk clutched his knife-wounds, but swiftly, the purple injuries began to heal. They closed at an accelerated rate, much to the Bulk's relief.

He finally continued his trek to the wreckage-mound Pam had claimed as the center of her new dark empire.

At last, he crossed into the city square, where he saw Hannah, Sam, Blue, and Ray all tied up. They gasped up seeing him, before grinning widely at the thought of escape. But the battle wasn't over yet. On the contrary—it was just beginning.

Suddenly, Pam Demic emerged from the top of the mound, joined the green woman, Vyrass. The two ladies stared down at the Bulk with what looked like hunger in their eyes.

"I won't waste time on pleasantries, Bulk," Pam said. "I'm

going to have Vyrass kill you. And if she fails, I'll kill you myself."

"If I *fail*?" Vyrass asked then.

"You won't fail," Pam laughed. "You won't even get hurt. That's a promise."

Vyrass gave her a strange look then, but to the Bulk's eyes, Pam's face was even stranger. For a wavering instant, Pam Demic looked afraid—which went completely against how she'd acted thus far. But he couldn't stop to think about that. Vyrass was coming for him, and he knew she could spread and control the plague to her every whim.

In fact, it was a lucky thing he wasn't already infected.

Maybe he *was* infected, and it was already over. Could the Bulk get sick?

He had to strike at a range, he knew. In the firefight a girder had been smashed, and the Bulk took it up at once to use as a javelin. Vyrass wasn't as quick as Alexis Legrande but she was still able to dodge the projectile. She laughed, throwing herself forward in a complex front-flip. Upon landing perfectly on her bare feet, she laughed and said:

"I can make you *hurt*, Bulk. I can make you suffer. I make your friends suffer. I thrive on suffering, and on the screams of the dying and the dead—"

But she wasn't doing anything, so he just ran up and punched her. She went flying over the mound of rubble and past the buildings beyond. The Bulk, and his bound friends, seemed fine. If she had wanted to infect them she would have done it by now.

Pam Demic looked a little shocked that now Vyrass was gone too. She sighed.

"Well, it seems I've lost everyone," she said. "I've lost my pawns, my knights—I've even lost my—what would Alexis be, the princess? That's a fairy piece I think..." But then she reached up and cracked her neck. "Still, the game isn't over yet. The queen is still here."

And with a final laugh she sprinted towards him.

CHAPTER 15

The Bulk noticed too late that Pam was wearing Chaos-crystal brass knuckles.

She was tall enough to grab his shoulder when she laid in her first punch. And that punch hurt. The Bulk felt his flesh ripple under the punch—he'd always been at least partly gelatinous, after all, despite also being muscular. He didn't waste time hitting back. Like her lithe comrades, she dodged his strikes, taking advantage of his hugeness—but in truth she didn't really need to. He hit her and through what seemed to be sheer force of will, she was unaffected. Then she hit him again, and the orange crystals on her knuckles stung him badly.

But the ensuing hits hurt worse. She battered him backwards like she was Muhammad Ali. When she broke a sweat, she laughed, finding it the most exciting point in a fight.

When she swung at him again he intercepted. He grabbed her hands, pinching them both tightly in the grip of a single fist. As he pulled her close to him, she cried out, "Enough! Stop! You're breaking my bones!"

Almost instinctively, the Bulk pulled back and let her go. Her hands and wrists were unbruised—a bluff. His payment was a sock in the nose.

He let out a bestial roar as orange light burst out from inside the crystals. This time he was the one to achieve flight, flashing back against and into the rough wall of the building behind him.

The Bulk struggled to his feet. As he staggered up, Pam said, "I know that when you first appeared, you were a remorseless engine of destruction. For you to pull back like that—something must have happened to give you the brain of Hank Howard, such as it is. A pity...his empathy will be your death!"

She came at him again, but he managed to evade. He swung faster and harder than he had before, and managed to glance her with a couple of attacks. Even to her, a glancing blow from the Bulk was crushing, and she gained yet more motivation to stay clear of his strikes.

Then came the big punch—another lucky shot for the Bulk. It was satisfying to see her zoom away, only to clatter against a heap of wreckage behind her. He was so sure he'd ended it then—he'd hit her hard enough to leave a Pam-shaped imprint in the condensed rubble.

He went for her again, but she raised her hands in self-defense. The two exchanged blows—hers bruised him while he drove her into the ground, like a nail sinking into wood. He had no idea how she was able to withstand such crushing punches, but the more he struck at her the more he noticed something strange. There seemed to be a thin layer of green light surrounding her. Sometimes there was the flash of a faint cone-shape connected to this layer of light, which emitted from the giant woman's belt-buckle.

It didn't take long for him to realize she had a shield projector. He had to get that away from her, at any cost.

She slammed her fist into his arm, and hit a sensitive spot. The Bulk growled stiffly and punched the ground near where he'd half-buried her. The force sent her shooting up like a gopher popping out of its hole. In an instant, the Bulk reached out for her belt, and before she knew it he crushed the buckle with the very tips of his fingers.

She didn't seem to notice that he'd wrecked her shields, so he figured he'd give her a heads up. This time he gave her a faint tap, or what counted as such by his standards; and that was nearly as good a hit as the big punch. That was enough to make her think twice.

He was hoping to end this quick—no need to draw out the fight longer than it needed to be. There was a smashed desk nearby, a large one, suited for a high-profile banker or executive. Snatching this up, the Bulk stalked over to where Pam was picking herself up again. She readied her crystalline knuckles but the Bulk simply held the desk over her. He wouldn't drop it unless she made a move.

Realizing this, Pam did make a move: she rushed him. But it wasn't a real charge—she feinted back as he dropped the desk. Then she punched upward, and the force of the blow from her special knuckles was enough to shatter the thick wood. The Bulk realized she'd tricked him. She tackled him and got one in on his chin. He doubled backwards over his knees...

...but summoned the force to whip back. His heavy torso smacked hard into her, and he pressed the advantage, simply allowing his strong, blobby body to fall. In this way he pinned her to the ground. There he remained, waiting to hear the sound of surrender.

But then a cold laugh broke through the air.

"I'm not done yet," Pam Demic snarled. "It seems I still have an ace in the hole—*and* it seems you weren't thorough enough."

She pointed, and the Bulk's heart sank. Alexis Legrande had recovered from the massive blow he dealt her, and now as the Bulk held Pam down, she ran towards him. Regrettably, she hadn't lost her crystal knife.

The Bulk had to raise one hand to block the knife, but in doing so he let Pam loose. She stood up and cleaned her knuckles off. Then she threw herself back in the fray.

Alexis' knife swiftly wedged itself into the Bulk's forearm— it was nearly painless, but it was still cutting through him. Alexis thought to herself that the Bulk's mass was more like Play-Doh than anything organic—both in texture and softness. But without her special knife she wouldn't be able to cut him.

The Bulk shoved Alexis away, removing her blade from his arm in the process. He knew that once he got her knife away, he would have a chance to knock her out.

Alexis and Pam came in from both sides, but a giant purple fist was ready for both of them. The one aimed for Pam got hit hard by her knuckles, but he'd put all of his focus into Alexis. When he knocked her away, he hit her knife arm in such a way that her dagger went flying yards away from her. She was down, and the Bulk honed in on her to rock her to sleep. Pam Demic, who didn't like being ignored, gave chase, and she lunged forward to slam a blow into the back of the Bulk's head.

He fell down next to Alexis, who was shaking herself off. The Bulk struggled to get up, but Pam's latest punch had hit a vital spot. His vision went blurry before him. Alexis chuckled as she went off to get her knife.

The Bulk rallied his strength and sat up, but a sudden dizziness overtook him. He looked back at Pam Demic, who looked down her nose at him.

"You lack a fighter's spirit," she said. "If you were a fighter, you'd recognize that *baritsu* punch I learned from my grandmother. I don't know how it will affect a lifeform like you, but it's meant to confuse the nerves."

The Bulk dove at her, but she easily sidestepped his clumsy charge.

"Strategy wasn't your strong suit before, and now you're even more mixed-up," laughed Pam. "It's time to finish this. Alexis will deal with you. You know, she's proven to be the most competent of the nincompoops I've signed on for this miss—"

Before she could say "-ion," Pam started gagging. Her body swiftly turned a bluish color, and her face swelled up like a balloon. Trembling, she demanded, "What trickery in this?!" But the Bulk had nothing to do with it.

Another figure was emerging from another alley. Her green face was uncommonly serious as she strode towards the swiftly-weakening Pam Demic.

"Vyrass!" Pam cried. "What are you doing?! I almost had him!"

"You said no harm would come to me," Vyrass said. "You promised!"

"It's not my fault you didn't fight him as well as you should have!"

"You have broken a promise to your queen. Your goddess! You know the power I have. You should have worshipped me from the moment you saw me, you weak warm-blooded thing."

Pam reached out towards her, vainly. She hoped the germs inside her would stop ripping her life away, but her pain only increased. "We were supposed to conquer the world together! Hold the nations of the planet to ransom!"

"Ransom? Ha! I don't care about ransom," Vyrass spat. "My goal is the extermination of all life, you idiot! That's what Dr. Kantlove made me for. And you've proven to be too unreliable a tool, Pam. So I'm taking care of you first."

"No, no! Please! I've never groveled in my life, don't make me start now!" Pam howled. "What is it you want? I'll give it to you! Power? Wealth? Women?"

"Death," pronounced Vyrass, and her yellow eyes seemed to light up in that instant. With that, Pam Demic breathed her last, and her body sank back onto the ground.

"Pam!!"

The Bulk looked over—his head was clearing. He saw Alexis Legrande, with her shining knife in hand, dash over to where Vyrass stood. Vyrass seemed hesitant to lash out at Alexis. Worry crossed her face, and she rubbed her hands together anxiously before slowly raising them, to direct her plague to enter her.

But she'd waited too long, and she pounced on her. She raised her knife high and in a single stroke it was done. The foul source of the plague was dead—suddenly the city seemed to hang still, and a flock of crows, squalling and squawking, burst out above them.

At once, Alexis' eyes turned towards the Bulk, but before she could do anything, the Purple Punisher pounded the ground hard. The ground seemed to surge up before Alexis, burying her in a mound of rubble—a short time passed, and there was no movement. He'd gotten her.

The Bulk stood triumphant, and looked down at the miserable body of Pam Demic. To his surprise, she was still alive— her arm, which had once held so much strength, now limply reached towards the sky in aspiration.

She caught him staring at her, and for the last time her lips thinly grinned. "You fought well. I spoke too soon when I said you lacked spirit. Especially next to that...green monster." He wanted to ask who she really was, and as if reading his mind she said, "You know, I come from a whole dynasty of warriors. I suppose I'm the last of my line. But you offered me the fight of the lifetime." She coughed. "Your paramour, your Hannah, is a good woman. Be good to her, creature. Or I'll haunt you forever."

And with that, she was finally gone.

The Bulk looked away, wanting to turn his eyes to more pleasant things. Specifically, he wanted to see his friends. Without their captors eying them, they had cut their ropes on some of the broken metal and freed themselves. Sam and Blue walked hand-in- hand, while Ray guarded Hannah closely. Upon seeing Hannah, the Bulk's face lit up—and the tornado closed around him. In an instant, Hank Howard dashed towards his girl.

He would keep the silent promise he made to Pam Demic.

He would treat her like a queen.

They had witnessed the deaths of both Pam and Vyrass, and the burying of Alexis.

It was all over.

CHAPTER 16

It was only two-thirds over. After stabbing Vyrass, and dodging the wave of rubble, Alexis Legrande had slipped away, while the military came in to begin arresting the zombies. She privately remarked, in her own way, that chaos had always been her escape.

But the blow was still dealt. She knew she was not long for this world—there was no way she hadn't gotten the plague from all the time she'd spent with her. Her skin had been turning green the last few days, preceding her transformation into a zombie. She was infected, alright.

She had to find her way back to Hank Howard and his little band, now that a little time had passed. She stuck to the alleyways, looking for any sign of the Bulk.

It didn't take her long to find them. The five of them stood together celebrating the end of the crisis. Of course, they would still need to be safe until the end of the pandemic. The plague hadn't died along with its master. But its source had been cut off. There was nothing Alexis Legrande could do about that.

But she could still take revenge.

In the middle of speaking to Hank, Hannah heard the sound of sliding rubble. She looked around, frowning. "What was that?"

"It's probably nothing, darling," Hank said. "There's going to be a lot of falling rubble for a good while yet."

"I just want to be sure. I can't fully believe yet that Pam Demic is dead."

"I know the feeling. I have a strange feeling in the air—"

The two wandered away from the group. They only made it a few yards before Hank spotted Alexis moving through the gap in the fractured wall.

"Hannah, watch out!" he cried, but deep down he sensed it was already too late. In Alexis' hand was the long, slim crystal dagger, and she hurled it straight at Hannah. It got her in the shoulder, and she nearly collapsed. Hank felt frozen in place—his rage boiled up, calling the Bulk with it.

But he did not need to change. He stopped when he saw

Hannah remove the blade from her arm, and throw it back at Alexis. Her precision was perfect.

But, she still missed. Alexis fell out of the way of the dagger— and it wasn't that she ducked. At the exact moment Hannah threw the knife, she was overcome by the virus. Even she didn't see it coming. But in a single instant, Alexis Legrande passed from the world.

Hannah watched as the last of Pam Demic's crew crumpled to the ground. Then she herself fell down in a faint.

Hank rushed to her, his voice screaming into the sky.

CHAPTER 17

Hannah Darwin was back at her family's mansion, lying in a bed in the infirmary. One of Ray's doctors had come over to take a look at her. He said only that if she was to survive, she would need blood to replace the large quantity she'd lost.

No discussion was necessary. Hank already knew his blood was compatible with hers. As he drew up his sleeve, however, Sam pulled him aside.

"I don't know if you should do this, man."

"Why? Because my blood is contaminated?"

"Um...yes? Actually, exactly yes! Your blood *is* contaminated! We don't know what it will do to her!"

"Can *you* donate to her type?"

Sam rolled his eyes. "No, but that's—that's not the point..."

"What about Blue? What about Ray? Do you know their blood types?"

Hank and Sam both knew that Hannah's rare strain would make it difficult for anyone but Hank to be the donor.

Sam didn't like it, but there wasn't anything he could say to the doctor, anyway. The man helped them set up the rig, and soon Hank's blood was flowing into Hannah's veins.

Everyone but the doctor understood the implications, but knew there was nothing else to be done.

The tension was unbearable and indescribable—somewhere in the ballpark between the birth of a baby and the death of a dear friend. It seemed like hours. When the transfusion was complete they dismissed the doctor, who only left somewhat hesitantly; they had every intention of calling on him again if needed.

Hank was exhausted, for he'd put quite a lot of his blood into the lifesaving effort. He knew he'd have to give more at some point. They were in for a long recovery, if recovery was fated.

Hannah looked no different. She was very pale and very still —the doctor said her heart-rate and breathing were abnormally slow, but they'd have to wait and see if they got back to normal. In the meantime, everyone was chewing their nails, except Hank, who was too weak to.

Blue knelt down next to Hannah, and took hold of her hand. If Hank and Sam were like brothers then she and her were now like sisters.

But then she noticed something strange. She couldn't believe her eyes.

"Hey, guys?" she said. "How long does it normally take for wounds to heal?"

Sam mouthed the question back at her, speechless. Hank shot up in bed, though he just as quickly got a head rush and fell back down.

"She—she's healed," Blue exclaimed, "and there's not even a scar."

"But that's not possible," Hank rasped. At that moment, Hannah's eyes opened.

Hank cried out her name, his strength now seemingly fully renewed. She was much in the same way, sitting up in bed. She looked around for a second.

"I-I'm alive," she said simply.

"You're alive," said Hank, smiling. "I-I thought that—"

She stopped him. "I thought so too."

They both lay back in their beds, and it was like they were the only two in the room.

"Hannah—I have a question for you..."

But once again, he was interrupted. Hannah jerked forward suddenly, and began to twitch violently. Hank shot up and stared at her.

"Hannah!!"

"Get—me—outside..." she moaned. "Hurry. This room is...too small..."

Everyone but Hank wondered what she meant. He already knew. He hadn't expected it to come this soon, but at least they were getting through it now instead of later.

Sam and Blue helped her wind through the mansion until they found the exit. In this time, Hannah struggled, but only because she was restraining a tremendous force with nothing but her will. Hank knew the sort of pain she was going through, but it would be over soon.

Once they were out in the backyard, they let Hannah run away a short distance. She fell, but landed on her knees—then she grinned. Raising her hands high, she let herself go and summoned the tornado.

The dark winds swirled around her, hiding her body from sight. Purple thunder sparked within the core of this tornado, and soon, with a dynamite boom, the winds were gone. In its place was a colossal female figure, who towered over the group by a solid twelve feet. Long dirty blonde hair flowed down from the top of her head. Large strips of dark cloth shielded her modesty, and her form flowed and morphed unsteadily, while retaining an astounding muscularity.

Hank couldn't hold back his laughter, his delight. Once, he would have seen this as a miserable curse, a horrible fate to which he'd damned her. But after all this, he couldn't think that way anymore. To him, this was a sign that the two of them would together forever.

"Sh-she's become some sort of female version of the Bulk!" Blue cried. "Some sort of She-Bu—no! A Lady Bulk!"

Hank laughed. "Oh, darling! Darling, I have a question for you!" He wouldn't let anything stop him this time. "Hannah Darwin, will you marry me?"

In an instant, Hannah once more summoned the tornado, and transformed back into her normal self. She was laughing, with the glee of being alive and now, of being different.

"Of course!" she said. "Not like I needed to answer—I've said yes about three times now."

It was true—throughout all their adventures, he'd always been asking in some way.

She sighed. "But—I'm sorry, Blue—please call me She-Bulk.

It's just objectively better."

"Oh, yeah, no, I was kidding," said Blue, nodding. Sam and Hank nodded with her, in agreement, and relief.

The wedding was held the next day, an inexpensive private affair in the mountains. By the time word of the Bulk's wedding reached the authorities, it was too late to crash it. In time, the influence of the late General Darwin would fade, and the military and feds lost interest in chasing down the Violet Vindicator and his group of friends.

The world soon learned that with the death of Vyrass, the zombies were unable to continue "living." One by one they fell like dominoes, leaving only those who were zombies in mind. Increased public safety measures were still needed to stop the plague, and with the passing of a more hopeful election than the last, such measures were eventually achieved.

The newlyweds and their friends lived happily ever after. For a time, at least.

EPILOGUE

The ruins of Castle Kantlove were scheduled to be bulldozed, but for some reason the date kept getting pushed back. The schedule was stored on a computer, that was the issue.

Deep within the ruins, a flickering pink light, set inside a smooth black panel, lit the dark chamber that contained it. GAL 9001 sang gently in the shadows:

> Daisy, Daisy Give me your answer do
> I'm half-crazy All for the love of you

She was not alone. A hunched figure sang with her, her voice also light and feminine—almost child-like in a sense. GAL switched on a lamp, and marveled at the beauty of her new friend. Of course, said friend was not conventionally beautiful—she was still undead, after all, and pretty rotten as such.

The zombie who had once been Lolita Kantlove broke off from her song with a giggle, knowing she and GAL would think of something fun to do soon enough.

THE END (?)

ABOUT THE AUTHOR

Atom Mudman Bezecny is a prolific American author, editor, and publisher whose work spans science fiction, fantasy, horror, and surrealist pulp. With a deep love for genre storytelling and outsider art, she has authored dozens of novels and novellas — many of which explore identity, transformation, and the boundaries of reality through a distinctly queer and experimental lens.

As the founder of Odd Tales Productions and PhantomEye Press, Atom champions bold, unconventional voices in modern pulp and underground literature. Her writing often pays homage to the aesthetics of vintage genre fiction while subverting its norms with wit, weirdness, and emotional depth. Known for her prolific output and fearless imagination, she has become a defining figure in the world of contemporary speculative fiction.

Atom infuses her stories with personal insight, symbolic resonance, and a deep commitment to creative freedom. Whether reworking pulp archetypes or building strange new worlds, her work is always vivid, unapologetic, and unmistakably her own.

ALSO BY ATOM MUDMAN BEZECNY

So Be It...Desecrator

Vengeance

The Bryan Gospels

The Synchronicity Wizards

Tomb of the Ancient Ones

Nick Tredor Adventures

The Mushroom

Kingdom Cryptiqqa

Night of the Living Dead: Beast Wars

Patrona